WOLF CALLED

THE LAST SHIFTER #2

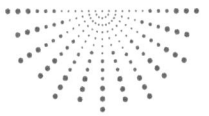

SADIE MOSS

Copyright © 2018 by Sadie Moss

All rights reserved.

No part of this book may be reproduced in any form or by any electronic or mechanical means, including information storage and retrieval systems, without written permission from the author, except for the use of brief quotations in a book review.

This is a work of fiction. Names, characters, organizations, places, events, and incidents are either products of the author's imagination or used fictitiously. Any resemblance to actual persons, living or had, or actual events is purely coincidental.

For More Information:
www.SadieMossAuthor.com

For updates on new releases, promotions, and giveaways, sign up for my
MAILING LIST.

CHAPTER ONE

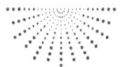

Thick straps dug into my skin, pinning me to a smooth, hard surface.

A metallic taste coated my tongue, like blood and bile all rolled into one. My skin felt numb, and the straps across my chest, waist, and legs were so tight it was hard to breathe. Flashes of light pulsed behind my closed eyelids, but I couldn't seem to drag them open. Whatever amount of strength it would take to perform even that small action was beyond me at the moment.

The thing I was strapped to swayed gently beneath me like a ship rocking on an open sea as a low hum filled my ears.

No. This isn't right. I shouldn't be here.

Something was wrong. *Everything* was wrong.

The fuzzy feeling in my body invaded my brain too, making me feel like half a person, a faded photograph of someone who had once existed. Someone who'd had hopes, dreams, losses, loves—though no one could guess what those were anymore.

"How many did Nils round up?"

The male voice came from somewhere near my feet.

"Eh, not as many as he wanted. The wolves scattered into the woods as soon as we moved in on 'em. Those fucking animals are smarter than I thought," another voice answered. This one was male too, and it had a deep rasp to it, as if the speaker smoked a pack a day.

"That why he stayed behind?"

"Yeah. He'll do a last sweep and snag any that are still hiding within the perimeter we set up."

A third man snorted. "Jesus. He'd keep hunting them forever if he could. He lives for that shit. But it's over, right? We got her. That was our main objective."

"It's over when Nils says it's over," the man by my feet joked. "He'll grab at least a few more before he gives up. Like you said, he loves the fucking hunt."

The three voices grated in my ears, and I wished I could lift my arms and press my hands to the sides of my head. Their casual, callous speech poked at a tender hole in my heart—one I couldn't quite identify yet. What were they talking about?

Nils? Who was that? And who was he hunting?

Questions floated across the surface of my dazed mind like scum on a brackish pond, but I didn't really want answers to any of them. A part of me knew the answers would split my soul wide open, so I clung to the numbness instead.

But the numbness was fading.

My brain was clearing, and as it did, my body grew more and more uncomfortable. My head rocked back and forth on the hard surface beneath me, sending pain shooting through the back of my skull.

I groaned, a low, pathetic sound that fell from my mouth before I could stop it.

The casual conversation around me stopped.

"Shit. She's coming out of it. Check her straps," the raspy-voiced man said.

"I did. They're good," the one by my feet answered.

But despite his words, hands grasped the leather binds holding me, cinching them even tighter, making me feel as if I were being slowly crushed to death. I moaned again, a pained, panicked sound.

"It's all right, Alexis. It's okay."

The new voice was soft, feminine... and familiar.

With agonizing slowness, I dragged my eyelids open, turning my head a little to peer toward the source of the sound.

Relief flooded me.

I knew those light brown eyes, would recognize them anywhere. I knew the brown hair sprinkled with gray, the simple bob haircut, the glasses. I knew every line and curve of the face staring down at me.

"Mom?" I croaked, hope rising in my voice.

The woman's expression twitched with surprise, then she shook her head slightly, and her features hardened. The mouth I'd seen smile so often compressed into a thin line. The crow's feet around her eyes deepened as her brows drew together. Those little actions changed her entire appearance, and I blinked, confused.

Why was my mom so angry? What had I done? And why had she let these men strap me down to a table, binding me so tight it felt like I was dying?

"Mom, I—"

Her face reacted to that word again, and the man stationed near my feet scoffed under his breath. I broke off, fear and panic worming their way into my foggy brain.

What was happening?

"Give her more sedative," my mom said, her voice thick with some emotion I couldn't identify. When the man by my feet hesitated, she looked up at him sharply. "Now!"

The big man shook his head. "Sorry, McGowan. Doctor Shepherd said not to give her too much. He doesn't want it interfering with her change. She's close."

McGowan? That's not her name. It's Maddow. Karen Maddow.

A dull pain beat at my temples as I tried to get my sluggish brain to work faster.

My mother glared at him. "She can handle a little more. You can tell him it was under my orders if you're so worried about it."

"All right, all right. Your fucking funeral." He abandoned his post near my feet, crossing to the other side of the room.

No... not a room. An ambulance.

We were in something that resembled an ambulance, although the space was bigger and more empty of equipment than others I'd seen. The movement of the vehicle as it sped down the highway was the cause of the rocking motion, and two of the male voices I'd heard must belong to the two guys sitting up front.

I was strapped to a metal gurney set up along one wall midway between the front seats and the back doors. Medical equipment was stashed in a cabinet attached to the other wall, and several guns and other weapons rested on a rack nearby. A clipboard with papers bearing spreadsheets hung from a hook behind the driver's seat. The interior of the ambulance was dark—there were no windows along the sides, so the only light came from the front and two small windows at the back.

This wasn't a *real* ambulance. At least, it wasn't like any ambulance I'd ever been in before. It looked too sparse, too makeshift for that.

This is all wrong.

I glanced back at my mom as the man dug into the medical supplies. A thought was pressing at the back of my mind, hovering on the edge of my consciousness like a tumor growing in my brain. Something important.

"Mom," I rasped. "What are you—?"

And then I remembered.

Like a video set on fast forward, every memory of the past few weeks came rushing back in to fill the void the drugs in my system had created.

The attack on the Strand complex. The panic, chaos, and confusion. The four men who claimed they would rescue me.

My mother, leveling a gun at my head and firing.

I sucked in a breath, my eyes widening, my chest straining against the thick leather strap that held me down.

"No... You—!"

Before I could get out more, the assault of memories continued, robbing me of speech.

Those four men *had* rescued me, saved me from a life of lies and cruel manipulation. I had run with them, all the way across the country, searching for some hope, some aid. For the Lost Pack.

But we'd been hunted.

Sometime during my ten-year stay in the Strand complex, they had implanted a microchip under my skin. And when I escaped, they'd used that chip to track me down like an animal. I'd been forced to flee through the woods, driven away from the men who had come to mean everything to me.

And this woman. The one whose face had seemed so familiar? I didn't know her at all.

"You're... *not*... my mother."

The words came out stilted and harsh as an anger like nothing I'd ever experienced flooded my veins with molten fire.

"Sanders, where are you with the goddamn sedative?" She held out a hand, palm up, but her gaze never left my face.

"I'm coming, I'm coming. Fuck, calm down."

"Give it to me. Now." The woman who wasn't my mother spoke slowly, as if she were addressing an idiot.

But I could barely hear her words. The rage burning through me lit up my nerve endings, feeding strength to weak muscles and making blood rush in my ears.

"*You lied to me!*" The scream tore from my throat, every bit of anguish and betrayal I'd experienced at the hands of this woman—of *all* of them—coating my words with venom. "How could you fucking do that? You made me think— You told me—"

"Sanders. *Now.*" The familiar stranger's expression didn't change, but her nostrils flared and her hand shook slightly.

Seeming to steel herself, she reached for me and smoothed my hair back with her fingertips, humming a soft lullaby. The song she always used to sing when I was sad or upset.

Our song.

The sweet, melodic sound twisted a knife in my heart, making me gasp for breath. I jerked my head away from her touch.

"No! Don't fucking do that! I thought you loved me! *You lied to me my whole fucking life!*"

My voice rose with each word, and I bucked hard against the straps restraining me, wrenching my head back and forth as I fought to free my arms and legs. The restraints held fast, but the entire gurney wobbled beneath me.

"Shit! Here, here!"

Glancing at me with wide eyes, the big man pawed through the supplies, grabbing a syringe filled with a pale amber liquid. He stepped up to McGowan, the woman I'd once loved like a mother, slapping it into her waiting palm. She yanked the cap off, bending over me to slip the needle into my arm.

There was a stab of pain like a wasp sting, and I renewed my struggles, jerking and writhing as I panted like an animal.

My not-mother's face contorted with concentration, and she bore down hard on my arm with her free hand, holding me still as she administered the drug. Her glasses slipped down slightly, and she wrinkled her nose to try to push them back up on her face—something I'd seen her do hundreds of times in the years I had known her.

That little gesture, that achingly *familiar* sight, broke my heart more than anything else.

I forced saliva into my dry, cottony mouth and spit in her face.

"Damn it!"

She jerked backward, yanking the needle out of my arm with another painful sting. Tossing the empty syringe into a basket behind her, she pulled her glasses off and wiped them on her shirt, then ran a hand down her face.

A muscle in her jaw ticked as she slipped the thick frames back on, but she seemed to relax a little now that the sedative was in my system. I could already feel it spreading through my veins, bringing the numbness back with it.

"I did care about you, Alexis," McGowan said, her face impassive. "I know you don't believe me, but of course I did. We spent too many hours together for me not to get somewhat attached."

"*Somewhat* attached?" I choked out.

The sedative raced through my system, slowing my movements as I continued to struggle against my binds. I could feel it trying to soften my muscles, but the hot anger radiating outward from my stomach wouldn't let it. My entire body began to shake, limbs quivering and teeth rattling as rage overtook me.

"You. *Never*. Loved. Me." My voice shook with emotion as I forced the words out. "You don't love someone and keep them locked up. You don't love someone and lie to them about everything. *Use* them as part of your sick experiments. That's not. Fucking. Love!"

"It doesn't matter." The woman with the simple bob haircut shook her head tiredly, as if she was already sick of having this argument with me. "It's over now. No more pretending."

My body jerked and twitched as it fought against the sedative, my muscles beginning to gain strength rather than lose it.

"*No!*" I screamed. "*You don't love someone and just give them up like that!*"

Burning tears ran down the sides of my face, hot streaks of anger and pain that disappeared into the wild mess of my dyed-blonde hair. A sound halfway between a growl and a whine rose in my throat, and my lips curled back from my teeth.

McGowan blinked and backed up a step, fear passing over her face.

Some primal part of me saw that fear and liked it. Wanted to hunt it down, to feast on it.

"What the fuck is going on back there?" the driver called from the front.

"Shit. Why isn't she going down? The syringe I gave you

had the max dose!" The big man beside me turned to my mother, his eyes wide in his broad, squashed face.

"Give me another," she ordered, her voice shaking.

"But—"

"Another!!"

He scrambled to obey, lunging toward the medical supply cabinet and digging out a second syringe while my mother reached for a gun on the wall behind her.

I could sense the fear rising in both of them, feeling it radiating from the front seats, and it fed the feral, wild *thing* that lived inside me.

The animal.

The wolf.

My body jerked again, but this time, I felt my bones break. White-hot agony filled me, and I screamed, arching against the tight restraints, the veins in my neck feeling like they would rupture.

"Motherfu—"

The man with the syringe moved toward me, needle poised, just as my mother raised her weapon.

But they were both too late.

With a howl, my wolf burst forth.

CHAPTER TWO

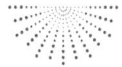

It hurt.

It hurt so fucking bad I couldn't think about anything else, couldn't focus on anything but the pain. The shift consumed me, destroyed me, burned me to ash like a phoenix before it rises from the flame.

Inside my skin, my bones cracked and reformed, growing larger and stronger. Fur sprouted all over my body as my mouth, nose, and ears elongated. The endless scream pouring from my lips morphed into a wild howl, the fearsome sound echoing off the metal walls of the makeshift ambulance.

The pressure of my sudden shift snapped the buckles of my restraints. They fell away, hitting the sides of the gurney with sharp pinging sounds. Disorientation and pain clouded my brain as the shift completed, and my large paws scrabbled for purchase as I tried to flip over. The gurney tilted to the side just as a shot rang out, and the bullet from McGowan's gun grazed my ear as I spilled onto the floor.

"No! We're supposed to keep her alive!" someone yelled from the front.

But the woman with the streaks of gray in her hair wasn't listening. Fear and panic filled her expression as she raised the gun again, pointing it right at me.

My wolf didn't let me hesitate.

It didn't even let me think.

I lunged toward her in the small confines of the vehicle, front paws striking her shoulders and bringing her down with a hard thud. She was a big woman, much taller than I was in human form. But right now, pinned beneath my massive paws and the weight of my lupine body, she felt small.

Vulnerable. Like prey.

Breathing heavily, she tried to raise the gun again, but my jaws snapped out, closing around her forearm. Coppery blood painted my tongue, and she shrieked in pain, thrashing beneath me as her suddenly useless fingers dropped the weapon.

The sound of her scream made my ears prick and my hackles rise, fed the fearsome predator that had overtaken my body and mind.

Prey.

I'd seen Noah's wolf kill a man once, seen how easily it could be done. But it hardly even mattered. My wolf knew what to do without needing any demonstration. She carried that ancient instinct deep in her DNA.

With a feral snarl, I dropped my head, clamped my teeth around the woman's throat, and tore.

Blood sprayed in a wide arc across the side of the

ambulance as her scream cut off abruptly, her body falling limp beneath me.

I stared down at her for a moment, trying to feel... anything.

But Alexis, the person I'd been all my life, the one who had once loved this woman, was buried so far beneath the surface it was like peering out through a window from miles away.

I wasn't in charge. Of any of this. The predator that had lain dormant inside my body for years, fed and nurtured by whatever concoction of drugs the Strand doctors had given me, had finally torn her way free. And she was in control now.

Everything appeared different through the eyes of my wolf. Colors, shapes—*nothing* looked familiar. Scents had become sharper, sounds more pronounced, as though the world itself was assaulting me with sensations. The pain of my shift had faded, but my body felt foreign, like it was no longer my own.

Then new sounds filtered into my ears. Raised voices from the front seat, and the harsh breathing of the man behind me.

No. The man attempting to *sneak up* on me.

I turned swiftly, the movement awkward in the confined space that seemed to have shrunk when I shifted. The man had his hand outstretched and his thumb poised on the plunger of the syringe. With a growl, I grabbed his forearm between my teeth, whipping my head sharply to the side and yanking him off balance.

He yelled and stumbled across the gently rocking ambulance floor, almost tripping over the corpse of the woman lying in a pool of blood near the back doors. The needle fell from his grasp, sliding across the blood-slicked floor.

"Fuck. Fuck!"

His eyes darted back and forth in his broad face, searching for some escape as he cradled his injured arm to his chest, his other hand groping blindly on the wall beside him for a weapon. He didn't seem to care about the driver's directive not to kill me any more than McGowan had.

"Sanders!" the man in the driver's seat called. "Initiate takedown protocol!"

"*You* initiate takedown protocol!" he shrieked, his voice rising with each word as beads of sweat trailed down his face. "There's a giant fucking wolf back here. She killed McGowan! Fucking help me!"

"Goddamn it! Go." The driver jerked his head at the man in the front passenger seat, who unclipped his seat belt.

Shit. I couldn't let them box me in.

As the man slipped between the seats into the back of the ambulance, I sprang into action. The one in front of me had finally wrapped his shaking fingers around a gun, but before he could drag it from the rack and fire, I was on him, teeth tearing at muscle and flesh. He screamed and jerked, his limbs flailing uselessly as he tried to fight me off. When he finally went limp, I threw his body aside.

Blood coated my muzzle and fur as I spun around, facing the new threat. This man's light blond hair shone like a stalk of wheat in the sun, an almost unreal hue to my new wolf eyes, as he stared in horror at the carnage around us.

Almost too late, he shook himself, rousing from his shock just as I lunged toward him. This man was faster than the others. He threw himself to the side, dodging my heavy paws and snapping teeth. I slammed into the back of the passenger seat, rattling the entire thing before I righted myself and shook out my fur.

When I turned around, the barrel of a gun was aimed at my head, mere inches away from my face.

"Don't. Fucking. Move," he commanded as he backed away slowly, shoving the gurney aside to put more space between him and me. "You got that? You understand me, *wolf?*"

The man couldn't have been older than thirty, and his breath came in shaky pants as he gripped the gun so hard his knuckles turned white.

"Orazio? You got this? Everything under control?"

The driver raised his voice from the front, craning his neck to look over his shoulder. The vehicle wobbled unsteadily, and he jerked the wheel to correct our course.

"Yeah." The golden-haired man blinked sweat out of his eyes, licking his lips nervously. "Yeah, I've got this. She won't do anything stupid."

He braced his legs wide to keep his balance as we sped down the highway, keeping the gun in his left hand trained on me. I stared at him, my predator's eyes taking in every sign of weakness, cataloguing every possible opening. He was of average height, but I could almost look him straight in the eyes as we squared off in the confines of the wide ambulance.

How big was I? All the wolf shifters I'd seen so far were larger than wild wolves, but I seemed even more massive than I remembered them being.

"Orazio! There's a tranq gun on the wall near the back door," the driver called.

"I don't fucking know, man. I think we should just waste her. We'll tell 'em it was an accident."

Wild fear gleamed in the man's eyes, and I saw his finger twitch on the trigger. He didn't care one bit about finding the tranquilizer gun or preserving me for Strand. He just wanted to live through this.

So did I.

His finger squeezed tighter as he moved the gun incrementally to the right, trying to line up the perfect shot right between my eyes. The vehicle jerked again as the driver turned back to look, and the blond man's arm dipped. In a flash, I threw myself forward. A gunshot rang out like a thunderclap in the small space, and a piercing pain tore through my side a half second before my massive body slammed into his.

The man grunted as we hit the blood-slicked floor of the ambulance and struggled frantically to slide out from under me. He freed his arm, raising the gun again, but I batted it away with a large paw. Another shot rang out, followed by a pained grunt, but I hardly registered it as my jaws closed around his throat. I felt his neck snap between my teeth, and his body stiffened and jerked before going limp.

As I crouched over his prone form, I realized his dark shirt was soaked with both his blood... and mine. The first shot he'd fired had hit me in the side, and blood pulsed from the wound, making me dizzy. I let out a plaintive whine, shaking my head against the pain and the sedatives still trying to overtake my system.

I couldn't rest. I couldn't stop. There was still one more. The driver—

The ambulance shuddered suddenly, rocking back and forth. I staggered away from the blond man, looking toward the front as I regained my footing.

The driver was slumped over the steering wheel, blood trickling from a bullet hole in the back of his head.

Oh fuck.

Oh no.

The man had dark skin and considerable bulk, and the weight of his body on the wheel was the only thing keeping it from turning of its own accord.

I glanced out the window quickly, fear closing my throat. We were on a stretch of highway that was straight and narrow, a two lane road bordered by wide ditches and thick woods on either side. But without someone controlling the large vehicle, it was only a matter of seconds before we drifted into one of the ravines on the side of the road.

A loud groan filled my ears as the ambulance listed to the right, hitting the rumble strips on the side of the road before shifting away again. My heart rose in my throat, and I loped toward the front seats, the wound in my side making my gait uneven.

Shit!

There was nothing I could do in this form except watch the landscape outside zoom toward me, the yellow and white stripes on the gray-black road racing by in a steady stream. I couldn't get out of here, and I couldn't stop the runaway ambulance.

I watched, helpless, as death bore down on me.

CHAPTER THREE

All those hours I'd spent searching inside myself for the wolf I wasn't sure existed hadn't prepared me for how overwhelming the shift would be—how complete. The animal had overtaken my body and mind, and even as my wolf whined plaintively, begging me to find a way out of this, she refused to cede control.

Please. You've done enough. You need to let me take over. Please!

I strained to force my wolf down, pushing for the shift with all my might as the wheels rolled over the rumble strips again, and the vehicle trembled and rocked. My paws slipped on the puddles of blood spreading slowly across the grungy metal floor.

A sudden realization penetrated my swirling mind as I stared in dread out the front windshield: I would never see Noah, Rhys, Jackson, or West again. Never see the four shifters who had stormed into my life in a hail of gunfire and saved me from a life I hadn't even known I needed rescuing from. The ones who had shown me what it meant to truly be alive, who'd taught me the meaning of family in a way that woman Strand had paid to masquerade as my mother never could.

The thought pierced my heart, hurting almost worse than the bullet that had pierced my side.

No!

That couldn't happen. I *had* to get back to them.

I needed to see Rhys's beautiful, tortured blue eyes. Hear Jackson's laugh. Feel Noah's arms wrapped around me, sheltering me from everything awful in the world. I needed to taste West's lips on mine again.

My wolf let out a deep-throated howl, as if she missed them just as much as I did. As though her call could bring them back to us, somehow reuniting our little pack.

The ambulance veered across the yellow line, drifting toward the other side of the road as it rocked unsteadily. Icy fear flooded my veins.

Please, I begged her, my snout wrinkling in a snarl as I fought with everything I had in me. *Please, let go!*

And finally, she did.

I doubled over as the shift wracked my body once again, sweeping through me like a seismic quake. My agonized howl morphed into a ragged scream as my limbs reformed in a human shape, and I fell to my hands and knees, one hand reaching up to clutch at the bleeding hole in my side. A small piece of metal protruded from it, and with a groan, I pulled it out. The shift had forced the bullet from the wound.

The scent of blood wasn't as strong in this form, but the smell of it made my stomach revolt anyway. Retching and gagging, I forced myself to crawl through the sticky red pools toward the front seat. Hazy gray light edged my vision, and my limbs shook so much they could barely support my weight, but I clenched my jaw, my focus narrowing to a single objective.

Reach the driver.

Using the beat-up leather seat, I hauled myself up to stand, and when I looked out the windshield, my heart stopped.

I was out of time.

The ambulance barreled toward a curve in the road like a runaway train, and a shot of adrenaline forced my exhausted body into action. I yanked the driver's upper body off the wheel, shoving him to the side.

But he was too fucking big, and I was too fucking small. I couldn't get his weight to shift off the gas pedal.

"Damn it!"

Giving up on moving him, I jerked the wheel with one hand, trying to follow the curve of the road. But I overcorrected. I'd never driven any car before, let alone one this massive.

The wheel turned too fast, and the front tires veered sharply to the right. The back of the ambulance swung around in a wide arc, spinning me in a dizzying circle as the large vehicle tipped onto its side.

We hit the shallow ditch and rolled.

Time seemed to bend and stretch as the ambulance

tumbled over the uneven ground. Metal grated and screeched. The steering wheel was ripped from my hand as my body hurtled toward the ceiling then back to the floor. All the breath was forced from my body by the impact, and something snapped in my arm, sending sharp pain tearing through me.

I didn't know where I was, what was happening. It was like being at the epicenter of an explosion—nothing but sound and light and horrible, crushing force.

Then, with a sudden, sharp jolt, everything stopped.

Around me, the world went still and silent, and I wondered for a moment if I was already dead.

Then my lungs dragged in a painful gulp of air, as though I were a diver resurfacing after too much time underwater. Pain blazed through my body, coming from too many sources to pinpoint any of them.

My nostrils burned from the pungent scent of gasoline. The medical cabinet had spilled its contents everywhere, and the clipboard from behind the driver's seat lay near my face. Everywhere I looked, I saw red. The ambulance was upside down, and the lifeless bodies of the people I'd killed had been tossed around like broken dolls, painting the interior in sweeping slashes of blood.

I retched again, my body too weak to even heave properly.

I should've stayed a wolf. She was stronger than me. Maybe she could've lived through this.

My eyelids fluttered, my gaze sliding out of focus. But as

it did, two words on the stained paper in front of me caught my attention.

Sariah Walker.

Choking back my pain and nausea, I pressed up onto the elbow of the arm that wasn't broken, peering down at the wavering writing on the spreadsheet.

It was a roster. A list of Strand test subjects.

And there was her name, written in black and white and smeared with red, alongside the words *Patient #298. Salt Lake City, Utah.*

My lips quivered, emotion overwhelming me. She was still alive. She must be.

I had to get out of here—I had to tell Rhys.

Never mind that I was naked and nearly broken. Never mind that I had no idea where Rhys was, or how to get to him even if I did know. I'd watched him move heaven and earth to try to reach his sister, and if she was still alive, I would do everything I could to help him get her out.

But first, I had to live.

Dragging myself on my good arm, I pulled my battered body over the slick surface of the vehicle's ceiling, making my way toward the broken window by the passenger door. The hood had popped open, hanging down over the windshield, and somewhere in the engine a fire had started. I had a sudden flashback of Jackson flicking a lighter open and torching the van we'd driven to Vegas in. The memory urged me to move faster despite the pain that nearly blinded me. I knew all too well how quickly the entire ambulance could go up if the gas fumes ignited.

A fallen tree branch had pierced the passenger side window, shattering the glass. I forced my body through the tight space that remained, trying to lift myself enough to avoid the shards that stuck out from the side of the frame. But they dragged against my skin anyway, drawing new cuts on my ravaged skin.

Finally, I hauled myself free of the ambulance. One arm hung limply by my side, swollen and bruised, and the wound in my side kept me from standing up straight. But I clambered to my feet, stumbling away from the smoking, blazing vehicle. It was painted black, not the usual red and white of an ambulance. The scents of blood and gasoline mingled in my nostrils, so strong I felt like they were seeping into my skin.

I couldn't stay near the wreck. I couldn't allow Strand to find me again, to take me back to Austin or who-knew-where. If I could get into the forest, maybe I could shift again—allow myself to rest and heal in wolf form. A cold spring breeze gusted through the trees, chilling my damp skin, and I wrapped my good arm around myself, wishing for the thick pelt of my wolf.

Just as I reached the tree line, a familiar whooshing sound came from behind me—and even at this distance, I felt the heat that blasted outward as the makeshift ambulance ignited, crackling flames sweeping over it. A wave of sorrow nearly bowled me over, and I leaned against the trunk of a tree to stay upright.

Mom...

But she wasn't my mom anymore. She never had been.

And the truth was, she'd been dead long before the ambulance caught fire. Before it crashed. But the finality of it, the destruction of even her corpse, made me mourn for something that was never real.

Keeping my good hand pressed to the wound at my side, I forced myself to turn away and move deeper into the woods. Rocks and twigs dug into my feet, but I hardly noticed that slight pain.

One foot in front of the other.

Just put one foot in front of the other.

But the mantra wasn't enough to counteract everything my body had been through. My feet dragged more and more, shuffling over the rough ground until finally, my knees buckled. I landed in a heap, dirt and leaves sticking to my blood-slicked skin. I kept my hand pressed tight to the wound in my side, though the bleeding had slowed.

My wolf had crawled back down deep inside me, as traumatized as I was. I willed the shift to come again, prayed for it, begged for it—but she refused to return.

Lying on my side, I curled up into a tight ball, shivering and shaking. A fuzzy gray light filled the edges of my vision, and my head hurt too much to keep my eyelids open. So I let them drift shut, allowing the quiet sounds of the forest and my shallow breathing to fill my senses.

I wouldn't die out here. I wouldn't.

I would just rest.

For a little while.

CHAPTER FOUR

I clung to the trunk of a tree with my good arm, staring back toward the road. Flames licked across the overturned vehicle, melting the tires that still spun in lazy circles.

There wasn't time. I had to run. I had to disappear into the woods.

But my body refused to move, and I couldn't tear my eyes away from the inferno before me. Then a sharp cry came from inside the ambulance, and my heart seized in my chest.

Someone was alive in there.

I hadn't killed everyone. Someone was still alive, trapped inside, burning to death.

The cry came again, louder this time and distinctly feminine.

"Sariah," I whispered.

I wasn't sure how I knew it was her trapped inside the wreck, but I did, without a doubt. I was sure of it.

Without even thinking, I started to stagger back toward the blaze, but before I got halfway there, my foot landed on something cold and metallic. With a loud snap, the sharp teeth of a bear trap sprang up, impaling my calf. I pitched forward, catching myself on my broken arm and screaming in agony as the bones cracked.

Moaning and gasping, I rolled onto my back, staring up toward the dark sky to find a pair of cool green eyes gazing down at me.

"That's how you take down a wild animal."

Nils grinned cruelly, dusting off his hands in satisfaction. He crouched over me, pulling a wicked looking carving knife from a sheath at his side. It gleamed in the light of the fire that consumed the ambulance.

Inside it, Sariah's screams had died. She had died. I'd failed her.

"Scruuuuubs!"

Noah's voice reached my ears, a faint call from a great distance.

I shook my head, staring up at the leering blond giant in horror.

No. My men weren't supposed to be out here. I couldn't let them yell like that. They'd bring the Strand hunters down on us all.

"Run, Noah..." *I choked out.* "Run."

"Scrubs!"

The voice was louder, more insistent.

Why wouldn't they listen? They needed to get away. Nils was here. He'd kill them, right after he killed me. I squeezed my eyes shut, anticipating the sting of his knife as it pierced my skin.

"Scrubs! Jesus fuck. I found her!"

This time, the voice was West's, thick with worry.

Hands brushed my skin, and my eyes flew open. I lashed out, trying to fight off Nils with the last of my strength, and pain shot down my arm when I moved. My feet kicked feebly, but the bear trap around my ankle had disappeared. It wasn't real. It never had been.

My feverish mind reeled, no longer sure what was a dream and what was reality. But the fingertips touching my face were gentle, and the musky scent that hit my nostrils was achingly familiar.

"Alexis. It's me," West whispered.

It was dark—that much of my dream had been true, at least—but I didn't need much light to see his inky eyes glinting like stars.

"West..."

I wanted to reach for him, but now that consciousness had found me again, so had the pain. My body hurt everywhere, and I was so weak I could hardly move. So I just stared up at him, trying to absorb every detail of his face in the heavy shadows, trying to convince myself this was actually real.

His hands didn't leave my face, but he glanced up, peering through the woods.

"She's here!" he called in a low voice. "And she's... she's hurt."

Three other figures burst through the trees, and even as I

struggled not to pass out again, my body reacted to their presence. It felt like I'd been living with a ten-ton weight on my chest, and as soon as I saw the four shifter men, it lifted, allowing me to draw a full breath for the first time since I'd woken up in that awful mockery of an ambulance.

"Oh fuck! Alexis!" Jackson threw himself to his knees on the ground beside me, his eyes wide and horrified as he took in my body. "What the fuck happened?"

I tried to speak, but I couldn't. The little burst of energy I'd gotten was fading already, and my eyes rolled back in my head again.

"The crash. She must've been in the thing when it rolled," Noah murmured, smoothing a hand over my hair. Even that hurt, but I didn't want him to stop.

"We need to get her out of here. She needs help."

West's comforting hands left my face, and then arms were sliding under my shoulders and knees, lifting me from the ground. I cried out, the pain rousing me once more, and West's breath hitched as he clutched me to his chest. I buried my face in the soft fabric of his shirt, trying to lose myself in the feel of him, the scent of him.

I was vaguely aware that I must look like a horror show—naked and covered in dried blood, purple bruises, and dirt—but I didn't care. West's skin against my skin as he carried me in his arms was the best thing I'd ever felt.

Although he tried to be gentle, every footstep he took jarred my body, sending pulses of pain throbbing through me. No one spoke as we made our way through the woods, or if they did, I was too out of it to hear what they said.

Some time later, we finally stopped. A door opened, and I was placed gently in the back of a car. Someone rested a blanket over me, and then a large body slid into the seat near my head, lifting it slowly so that my cheek rested on a warm, hard thigh. Someone else climbed in near my feet, and I shivered as the vivid memory of a bear trap snapping around my ankle washed over me.

That wasn't real. It was just a dream.

The thought was hardly comforting. I kept expecting to wake up from *this* dream any minute, to realize I was still alone in the woods, naked and exposed, dying slowly with no one to help me.

"Please," I whispered, the sound raw and choked. "Don't leave me."

"Fucking never." Rhys's voice came from above me, and I felt his fingertips ghost over my cheek. "Never."

"We need to get her looked at, man. She's banged the fuck up," Jackson said, his voice tight. He was the one sitting near my feet. "I think she's been shot too."

"Goddamn it." West slammed the driver's side door, and the car roared to life with a rumble. "We can't go to a hospital. We still have the IDs Carl made us, but I don't trust anywhere Strand might be able to track us down. It's a miracle we got to her before they did."

"Then where are we supposed to go?" Jackson demanded.

"Carl." Rhys spoke again, his voice rough. "He offered to help before. We need that help now. And he won't give us up; you know he won't."

"Yeah. Fuck, we're at least a couple hours away. Do you think she can make it?" Jackson's hands tightened on my ankles, and I shifted uncomfortably. He hissed a breath and immediately loosened his grip.

"Noah, pass us the first aid kit," Rhys said. "We'll do what we can."

There was some shuffling, and then Rhys leaned forward to take whatever Noah had handed back. They lifted the blanket away from my abdomen, and strong fingers cleaned the area around my wound. A bandage was pressed over it, wrapped so tight it made me gasp with pain, then Rhys's large hand came to rest over the whole thing, keeping pressure on it.

He leaned over, whispering into my ear, his voice invading the space where my mind drifted, somewhere between consciousness and sleep. "Hang on, Alexis. Please, fucking hang on. We just found you again. We can't lose you now."

Those words drifted around and around in my brain like tumbleweeds in a desert, causing a sharp sting in my heart that soothed as much as it hurt.

They had found me. Just like I knew they would.

Like they *always* would.

Because I was theirs. And they were mine.

CHAPTER FIVE

Warmth cradled me. A little cocoon made of soft cushions and smooth fabric. When I turned my head, the scent of lavender hit my nostrils.

I blinked slowly, squinting my eyes against the dim sunlight that penetrated the blinds on the windows. I was in a bed. A large, plush bed in a simple but tastefully decorated room. A few eclectic pieces of art hung on the walls, which were painted a soft cream, and a large dresser and closet took up one wall.

Where was I? This looked way too homey to be anywhere at Strand. Even the room I'd occupied for ten years in the Austin complex had maintained a sort of bland sterility that I'd never been able to erase, no matter how many personal touches I put on the place. But this place felt pleasantly lived in.

Why was I here? I dug through my memories, searching for clues.

The guys had found me. They'd carried me out of the woods, naked and covered in blood, and put me in a car, their bodies and voices tense with worry. I remembered some hushed conversation about where to go, but the only name I could recall being said was Carl's—and somehow, I didn't imagine he lived in a place as cozy as this.

Gathering my strength, I tried to sit up, noticing only when I did that I had an IV hooked to my left arm. Bandages wound around my bicep, covering the gashes the mountain lion had made. My right arm was in a cast, resting above the fluffy blanket that covered me. Someone had scrubbed the blood off my skin and dressed me in what looked like a hospital gown.

The door opened, and a woman walked in, eyes on her cell phone as she tapped out a message. When she looked up and found me staring at her, she paused. Then she quickly typed in another message on her phone before slipping it back in her pocket.

"You're awake," she said quietly, a sweet smile tilting her lips. She had wavy honey-blonde hair that fell past her shoulders, and the most open and honest face I'd ever seen.

I instantly wanted to like her, which also instantly made me wary. My track record for trusting the right people was only about fifty-fifty.

"Where am I?" I rasped, my voice scratchy as sandpaper. "Who are you?"

She crossed over to the bed, checking on the bag that hung nearby, feeding clear liquid into my IV. Then she sat on the edge of the mattress, gazing down at me with soft blue-green eyes.

"I'm Molly. I'm Carl's girlfriend."

My brows drew together. This wholesome-looking woman was dating the pawn shop owner with the cunning eyes and slicked back hair? The one who dealt in fake IDs and stolen cars and who knew what other kinds of illegal activities?

As if reading my thoughts, Molly chuckled softly. "Hey, we can't help who we fall in love with. The four horsemen brought you here. I'm a nurse, and I've helped out some of Carl's friends in the past when they've gotten into scrapes and couldn't go to the hospital. So the guys asked if I could take care of you."

Her use of the nickname "four horsemen" made me relax slightly. I remembered Carl addressing them by that monicker when we'd visited his pawn shop the first time. And if the guys knew and trusted her, that meant I could too.

"Thank you," I croaked. "Where are they?"

"They're with Carl. I texted him to let him know you're awake, so they should be back soon. In the meantime, how are you feeling?"

I paused, taking an internal reading. My arm throbbed gently, but the pain was like an almost-forgotten afterthought. I could feel a large lump on the back of my head, and my side ached every time I moved. But it was nothing compared to the agony I'd gone through in the ambulance. My memory of those events—including my shift—was fuzzy, but the one thing I remembered clear as day was how much it had fucking hurt.

"Good. I feel good." I nodded slowly, attempting again to sit up.

Molly chuckled, pressing me back down easily with one hand. "You're tough. I can see why they like you. But you don't have to put on a brave face for me. When they brought you in, you were..." She trailed off, a look of concern darkening her light eyes. "I don't know what you've been through, Alexis, but based on your injuries, it wasn't anything good. You fractured your radius and ulna, got a pretty bad concussion and several massive hematomas, and it's a miracle you didn't bleed out from the bullet you took in your side. You're going to be in recovery for a while, and you need to let me know how you feel. The truth."

"It hurts," I admitted, smiling in spite of myself. I liked this woman. She wasn't anything like the Strand doctors. "But it really is okay."

"All right. Well, if it gets—"

Before she could finish that sentence, the door burst open. There was a human log jam as Noah, Rhys, West, and Jackson all tried to enter the room at once. They finally all fell through the doorway, regaining their footing as they stopped to stare at me.

My heart swelled in my chest as I took them all in, and Molly glanced from them to me and back, a curious expression crossing her face. Then she rose from the bed.

"I'll... leave you all alone." She slipped past them, turning back at the door to look at me. "Call me if you need anything."

The door clicked shut behind her, but I barely noticed the sound. All my attention was focused on the four shifter men who stood before me, so different, and yet so perfectly matched. They complemented each other so well, and each of them complemented me, their strengths bringing out strengths in me I hadn't even known I had.

Noah stepped forward first. His blond hair was especially spiky and tousled, as if he'd been running his fingers through it repeatedly, and his beautiful face looked worn and drawn. The smile I loved so much was nowhere to be seen.

"Hey, Scrubs."

He bent over the bed and pressed a kiss to my forehead, letting the warmth of his lips linger on my skin for several seconds, as if he couldn't bear to pull away. When he finally drew back and looked down at me, I swore I could see the wolf that lived inside him behind his gray-blue eyes. My own wolf roused in response, and my nostrils flared as I breathed in his scent like I needed it to live.

Mine.

The word resounded in my head as I felt a sharp tug in my heart, and I couldn't tell if it came from my wolf or me. I wasn't sure it mattered. The only thing I knew was that it was the absolute truth, a fact so pure and basic there could be no doubting it.

I leaned up toward him just as he caught my face in his hands, staring into my eyes in shock. His full lips parted, and he let out a sharp breath. He'd felt it too. Whatever had just passed between us hadn't been one-sided.

"Holy fuck!" Jackson blurted, stepping forward. His head whipped back and forth between Noah and me, and I tore my gaze from Noah's mesmerizing, wide eyes to look up at him. "Did you two just—?"

Mine.

The same tug pulled on my heart, drawing me toward the dark-haired, wickedly handsome man. Jackson broke off, his jaw dropping open in an almost comical way. He snapped it shut, and his wide amber eyes searched my face as if trying to read something hidden there. He blinked.

"Ho-ly fuck..."

His voice was deeper and warmer this time, full of something that sent a shiver racing down my spine. His tongue darted out to wet his lips, and he shook his head in amazement.

Inside me, my wolf whimpered restlessly, happy but not yet satisfied. Noah sat back as Jackson drifted closer to the bed, the two of them staring at me in awed wonder.

My heart hammered in my chest as I shifted my gaze to Rhys, already sure what I would feel when I looked at him. His ice-blue eyes simmered with emotion as he stared at me intensely, his wolf hovering just beneath the surface of his skin. His shoulder-length black curls framed his face, making him look rugged and wild.

My she-wolf practically lunged toward him, and I jerked slightly on the bed, the word ripped from my lips this time.

"Mine."

It wasn't a question or a request.

It was a claim.

Given my past history with Rhys, I half expected him to sneer and turn away. Not that my wolf cared. She wasn't interested in silly little details like whether Rhys and I liked each other or not, whether the moody shifter sometimes drove me so crazy I wanted to smack him upside the head, or whether I'd ever get over my shame at his rejection in the woods. This was bigger than that—bigger than any human emotions or squabbles. It was a bond that couldn't be broken, couldn't be denied.

But to my surprise, Rhys's face softened, something like relief passing over his features. He stepped forward to rest his hand on the blanket covering my legs, his bright blue gaze locked on my face.

"Yours, Lexi."

A rush of emotion made my lips quiver as I finally turned toward West. His face was serious, his shoulders tense, and he watched me as if he couldn't quite believe what was happening.

The familiar feeling rose up inside me again, a need almost too deep to put into words as something in me called out to something in him.

Mine.

With that, the wild, dangerous wolf that lived inside me laid her last claim, whuffing in satisfaction as she settled back contentedly.

I stared into West's dark eyes, trying to gauge his response. I felt the tug of the bond pulling me toward him, like it would never truly be satisfied until we somehow became one. I wasn't surprised—I had known he would be my last. I'd felt the connection between us in the kiss we'd shared after we reached the Lost Pack, before everything went to hell. I had claimed him just as much as my wolf had, had wanted him just as much.

"You too, West," I whispered. "I need you too."

West shifted uncomfortably, and although heat flashed in his eyes, he fisted his hands by his sides, clearly fighting against it. His dark skin flushed slightly, and he tugged his full lower lip between his teeth.

"I'll just... go check in with Molly. Make sure she's got everything under control."

He ducked his head, scrubbing a hand over the back of his neck as he moved toward the door. When he reached it, he turned halfway back, glancing at me over his shoulder. I saw the same heat flare again in his inky irises, and a deep longing too. For a moment, his hand came off the door handle, and I thought he might stride over and crawl right up onto the bed beside me.

Then he blinked, swallowed hard, and left.

The door closed behind him, leaving a thick silence hanging in the room. My wolf twitched with anxious irritation as soon as he was gone, and I felt suddenly like an essential piece of myself was missing.

"Holy fuuuuuuck!" Jackson tipped his head back, letting out the last word like a howl. He looked back down, his eyes darting between the two remaining men and me as a wide, shocked grin split his face. "What. The. *Fuck*. Just. Happened?"

"I think you know what happened," Rhys growled, his gaze still burning into me with the intensity of blue flame. "Scrubs here just claimed each of us as her mates. And if I'm not mistaken, each of us claimed her back."

CHAPTER SIX

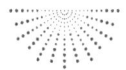

A mate bond.

That's what they called it.

I still wasn't sure exactly what it meant, what it entailed, or why my wolf had chosen four men to be my mates. According to the guys, that wasn't the norm among shifters—at least, as far as they knew. But then, almost nothing seemed to be normal about me. Not my upbringing, not the "elite facility" Strand had kept me in, not the size and power of my wolf. I had been a special experiment, something new for the doctors to test and analyze.

It was strange. I'd grown so close to the men over the last several weeks, falling for each of them in their own right, growing to care about them because of who they were.

But the mate bond intensified all of that, made feelings I'd been unsure of before as strong and clear as day. It was different than lust, different than love even. It was like they'd become a part of me, like a bit of my soul existed inside each of them, and I felt a constant tug to reconnect with those pieces of myself.

My wolf seemed utterly content with the whole situation, but as I lay awake that night, staring up at the ceiling, I wasn't sure I felt the same. It was all so much, so intense. I'd never even been on a date with any of these guys—or any date at all, really—and now they were my mates. I felt like we'd blown past several milestones I'd spent my whole life looking forward to.

In all my years hidden away in the Strand complex, I'd dreamed about what my life would be like when I finally got out.

I'd dreamed of romance.

Of falling in love.

I *hadn't* dreamed of bloody fights in speeding vehicles, or of having the animal that shared my body choose not one, but four mates for me.

Molly had removed the IV from my arm earlier, but I was still heavily dosed up with painkillers. They made me woozy and tired, but my churning mind wouldn't let me sleep. My arm and side throbbed dully, and I shifted uncomfortably, listening to the sounds of breathing and the soft snores that filled the room. Molly's house only had one guest room, but I was positive the guys wouldn't have wanted to sleep anywhere else even if she had a million rooms.

Hell, even if that was an option, I wouldn't have let them. I might not be sure how I felt about this new mate bond yet, but I couldn't deny that something inside me felt unsettled and anxious whenever these four were away from me. Even West had come back to sleep in here with all of us, although he'd spent the entire afternoon avoiding this room.

Why? What's going on with him, anyway?

I'd worried about Rhys rejecting me, but I'd never expected the cold shoulder to come from West. Not after the way he'd looked at me before he kissed me. Not after that kiss.

"Hey, Scrubs. Can't sleep?"

Noah's soft whisper caught my attention, and I looked over as he crept toward the bed. He lay down beside me, settling his large body carefully next to mine, careful not to disturb my injuries. He wore only a pair of shorts slung low on his waist, and even through the blanket, I could feel the heat of his skin.

I rested my head against the pillow, gazing into his warm gray eyes. "No. I know I should. I feel tired, and the drugs make me a little woozy. But I can't stop thinking."

He reached up to smooth a strand of hair away from my face, his touch achingly gentle. "About what?"

"About everything." A smile tilted my lips before it slipped away again. Then I swallowed, trying to organize my thoughts. "I shifted, Noah. In the Strand ambulance, or whatever it was. My wolf came out."

He nodded, his gaze full of understanding. "I thought you might've."

"Why?"

"Well, for one thing, when we found you, you were naked. I figured—well, hoped—that was the reason why. I couldn't stand to think of any other reason for it." His eyes darkened for a moment at the memory before his fingers found a lock of my hair again. "Plus, your hair is different."

"What?"

I craned my neck, and he held up the strands of my hair so I could see them. They were brown. Even in the dim light, that was obvious. I hadn't noticed before, but the light blonde color I'd dyed my hair had vanished when I'd shifted into a wolf and back. My hair had grown back in its usual color.

"Oh." I shifted my gaze to Noah. "Did you know that would happen?"

"Nah. You're the first shifter I know who dyed her hair." He chuckled ruefully. "So much for that disguise."

The IDs I'd gotten from Carl last time we were in Vegas had pictures of me with blonde hair. I could re-dye it, but Noah was right. It wouldn't be a very effective disguise if it returned to its original color every time I shifted. Not that it mattered. I wasn't sure there was a disguise in the world that would keep Strand from hunting me—from finding me.

"Noah." My stomach churned as I forced the words out. "I killed my mo—the woman pretending to be my mom. My wolf did. And the other people in the ambulance too. I don't... remember it all clearly. The whole thing is just flashes; bits and pieces, with whole chunks missing. I don't remember much of anything clearly until I woke up here. But I know I killed them all. I tore her throat out."

Pain flickered in his eyes, and he bit his lip, rising up on one forearm so he could gaze down at me. "I'm so fucking sorry, Scrubs. I hate that you had to do that. But she *wasn't* your mother. She wasn't on your side. And she would've killed you if it came down to it, you have to know that. You were defending yourself."

I twined the fingers of my good hand in the sheets, gazing up at him. "I know. I know that. It's just, what my wolf did—what *I* did as a wolf—none of it felt like it was under my control, you know? I felt... feral. Wild."

Noah tugged my hand away from the sheet, lacing our fingers together. "It's not easy. Some people don't even survive their first shift. Our bodies aren't equipped to deal with it at first. There are two halves of you now that have to reconcile with each other. It's harder for some people than others to find that balance. We all struggle with it sometimes."

I grimaced. "It felt like I was buried somewhere deep in her psyche. I finally understood how Rhys got lost in his wolf—why he couldn't shift back. It was like the wolf just took over who I was. She was so strong."

A look of concern flashed over his face, and he squeezed my hand. "You won't get lost, Scrubs. We won't let you. But your wolf does sound strong. Maybe it's part of whatever new experiment Strand was doing on you—why you were such a special test subject."

Fear trickled down my spine like ice water. Had they made me some kind of monster, some uncontrollable beast? I wasn't exactly sorry I'd killed those people in the ambulance, but it scared the shit out of me to acknowledge that I'd had no control over it. The predatory instincts inside me had been too strong to resist.

"Maybe that's why your wolf chose four mates," Noah mused, his gray-blue eyes narrowing thoughtfully. "The mate bond can have a stabilizing effect on a wolf. Maybe she needed that much support."

Dragging my gaze away from his face, I drew a deep breath. The contact between our hands, the feel of his thumb brushing my skin, the heat coming from his large, warm body next to mine—they all fed some primal part of my soul, sparking a need for more deep inside me. Every touch from these four men was like a drop in a bucket that would never, ever be full.

I needed all of them in a way that was beyond reason or logic. And Rhys had said each of their wolves had claimed me too. But I couldn't help but feel like I'd somehow forced this on them, like my uncontrollable she-wolf had ruined their pack dynamic. Would they really be okay with sharing me? The look in West's eyes when I'd told him I needed him too still haunted me.

"I'm sorry if I messed things up between you all. I didn't mean to... force myself on any of you. Is this really how the mate bond works?" I asked softly. "The wolf chooses, and then everybody just has to live with it, whether they like it or not?"

Noah lowered his chin a little, shaking his head. "No, it's not like that, Scrubs. And you don't have anything to be sorry for. The mate bond isn't like some decree handed down from on high. It's your wolf—who *is* a part of you, whether it feels like it right now or not—choosing her perfect match. And our wolves choosing her right back."

"So you're okay with this?" I asked, biting my lip.

His gorgeous smile tilted his lips, which hovered so close to my own, I could feel his breath on my skin. "I'll admit, I never expected to bond with the same female as all my pack mates. But what are we supposed to do? Fight against it? Fight each other for you? I'd rather die than do that."

"Do you wish your wolf hadn't chosen me?"

It was a dumb question to ask, maybe. It was like handing him a dagger and asking him to stab me in the heart with it. If he said yes, it would kill me—I wasn't sure I'd ever recover from the guilt and pain of that rejection. But I had to know.

Noah's gray-blue eyes warmed, crinkling slightly at the corners as his smile widened. "Didn't you hear what I said, Scrubs? My wolf is a part of me. It wasn't just him that chose you. *I* did. I think I chose you the first day I met you, when I saw how much hope you had despite everything you'd been through. I've never met anybody as strong as you."

A tear leaked from the corner of my eye as his words made my chest hurt and soothed the ache all at once.

"I chose you too, Noah. Before my wolf. Before the bond."

His smile seemed to radiate pure joy, and instead of answering with words, he dipped his head and pressed his lips to mine. I could feel him carefully managing the weight of his body to make sure he didn't disturb any of my injuries, taking care of me like he always did. His kiss was soft, warm, and exploratory.

My mouth opened, and our lips moved in perfect harmony as we tasted each other. He slid his tongue across mine in deep, even strokes. Nothing about this kiss was forceful or hurried, but it was so deep and languorous it felt like I might drown in it.

Despite my injuries and exhaustion, and the painkillers coursing through my system, an electric charge seemed to gather in my body, radiating out from my core. I disentangled my hand from Noah's, bringing it up to slide my fingers through the short-cropped hair on the back of his head, bringing him closer as our kiss became impossibly deeper.

I wanted to kiss this man for the rest of my life. I wanted his kisses for breakfast, lunch, and dinner. Fuck food. Who needed it?

Finally, Noah pulled back, breaking the contact of our lips and looking down at me with an expression that melted my insides. He pressed small kisses to the corners of my mouth before trailing his lips down my neck and over my collarbone and shoulder. He rested his head on the pillow next to mine, burying his face in the little nook where my shoulder met my neck and curling his large body around mine protectively.

"I will always choose you, Scrubs. Always."

He sighed contentedly, and we lay like that in peaceful, happy silence for a while until his breathing evened out and his body relaxed. I ran the fingers of my good hand over the strong muscles of his forearm, memorizing the feel of his skin.

Then I nestled deeper into the soft bedding, finally allowing my brain to slow down. My gaze moved around the shadowed room lazily, but it stopped on a pair of deep brown eyes that shone in the darkness.

West sat against the wall, elbows propped on his bent knees, watching me with an inscrutable look on his face.

CHAPTER SEVEN

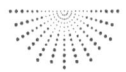

The bed dipped, rousing me from a dreamless sleep. Hazy morning light filled the room as I blinked, turning my head toward the movement and finding myself almost nose-to-nose with Jackson.

"Morning, Alexis."

He kissed the tip of my nose, making little tingles shoot across my skin like ripples on a pond. I was highly conscious of the fact that he was the only one of these four I hadn't kissed yet. I didn't know what it would be like, didn't know how those laughing lips would feel pressed against mine. But I wanted to find out. Desperately.

Noah stretched against my other side, where he'd apparently slept all night.

"What the fuck are you doing, Jackson?" he asked sleepily.

"Just thought this side of her might be cold, since you've got that side covered so well." Jackson snuggled a little closer to me, lifting his head to peer over my shoulder at his pack mate. "I seem to recall *somebody* saying we should give her some space—let her have a good night's sleep." He quirked an eyebrow pointedly. "Huh."

"How'd you sleep, Scrubs?" Ignoring Jackson's teasing words, Noah kissed my shoulder.

I smiled. "Good."

"See?" He cocked an eyebrow at Jackson, who muttered something that sounded like "no fair" under his breath.

"What the fuck are you both doing?"

Rhys rose from his pile of blankets on the floor, coming to stand at the foot of the bed with his arms crossed. His curly black hair brushed his shoulders, and just like the other two, he wasn't wearing a shirt. His sculpted muscles bunched as he crossed his arms over his chest.

The rest of the blanket piles on the floor were abandoned. West had already slipped out of the room, apparently, though I had no idea where he'd gone.

"Helping Alexis sleep," Jackson supplied, as he and Noah both turned their heads to grin at Rhys.

"Exactly." Noah grinned.

I suppressed a laugh at how quickly the two would-be rivals had joined forces, teaming up to take on Rhys. The black-haired shifter seemed to realize it too, because he rolled his eyes.

"She doesn't need your fucking shenanigans right now. She's supposed to be healing. Or don't you remember what an absolute fucking mess she was when we found her?"

At those words, I felt both of the men beside me tense,

and when I looked back at Noah, worry and pain reflected in his stormy gray eyes. They both moved to draw away, and I reached for them, trying to pull them each back toward me one-handed. The movement tugged at the stitches in my abdomen, and I hissed in pain, dropping my arm back to the bed.

"See?" Rhys glared at the other two.

"No! It's okay, Rhys. I wanted them here." My voice softened, and I shifted my gaze between Jackson and Noah, who looked so devastated to see me in pain that it broke my heart. "I'm okay. I feel... better when you guys are close."

"Are you sure?" Rhys pressed, a growl still lingering in his voice.

"Yeah. I'm positive."

Jackson looked around from where he knelt on the soft bedspread to my left. "In that case, we're gonna need a bigger fucking bed."

I laughed at that, then grimaced in pain again.

"Stop making her laugh!" Rhys ordered.

His bossy protectiveness only made me laugh harder, and I winced as my stitches twinged.

"That time wasn't me! That was all you!" Jackson leapt off the bed, holding his hands up innocently, eyes wide.

I snorted, more laughter bubbling from my throat. The tension and stress of everything that'd happened over the past few days needed some release, and maybe it was because the drugs made me a little loopy, but I couldn't seem to stop giggling.

Noah scrambled off the bed too, shifting his panicked

gaze between Jackson and Rhys. "Everybody stop making her laugh! Don't do anything funny!"

That only set me off again, and I clutched my side, trying to ease the strain on my stitches because it really did fucking hurt. But there was something so cleansing about it too. I'd needed this.

A knock came at the door, and Molly poked her head in as my giggles petered out. She glanced suspiciously at the three men before looking at me. "Do I even want to know what's going on in here?"

"Probably not," Jackson supplied with a grin.

She rolled her eyes at him, then stepped inside, followed by West and Carl, the man I'd met last time we came to Vegas. He was older than my men, probably in his early or mid-thirties. His dark hair was slicked back from his large forehead, and he had sharp features and clever eyes that didn't seem to miss anything.

"Put your clothes on while I take care of my patient," Molly said, shielding her eyes in mock-horror from Jackson's shirtless form. "Then—"

"Then we need to talk," Carl finished, his serious gaze sweeping the room.

All the joviality seemed to drain out of the air in a flash, and Jackson nodded. He, Rhys, and Noah left the room, and West hovered by the door while Molly approached the bed.

She asked me some questions about how I was feeling, took my temperature, and checked my head and the stitches on my bullet wound. By the time she was done, the three men had returned. She sat on the edge of the bed and laid a cool hand on mine as Carl cleared his throat, looking at the four pack mates.

"All right. Now I don't normally give a fuck what anybody gets into. We all have our lives, we all have our separate stories, none of my fuckin' business, right? But last time I saw you, I asked if everything was on the up and up here." He jerked his head toward me. "And you told me this girl was safer with you than she would be anywhere else. But the next time you bring her to me, she's got a gunshot wound, a broken limb, a concussion, and more bruises and scrapes than Rocky Balboa. So I gotta ask. What the hell kinda shit are you into here?"

All four of my men were silent, and in each of their eyes I saw a guilt I wasn't sure would ever go away completely. I could understand. There were plenty of things I hadn't forgiven myself for and probably never would. But I couldn't stand to see them look like that.

"They didn't do this. Any of it! It wasn't their fault," I said, struggling to sit up a little higher on the pillows. Molly helped me before stepping back to stand with Carl.

The dark-haired man shook his head. "Yeah, I didn't say it was, sweetheart. But I took on a risk letting them bring you here, and I need to know what the odds are of shit hitting the fan again. I don't want trouble showing up on my doorstep. I look after my woman, even if they can't do the same for theirs."

Rhys and West both looked murderous at the accusation, but Noah held out a hand to them before stepping forward.

"We understand, Carl. And we're more grateful than we

can say. To you and to Molly." He dipped his head in thanks, and she smiled softly. "We're almost certain we weren't followed. The people we're hiding from don't know where we are, and we don't think—" His gaze flashed to me for a second, and the space between my shoulder blades itched. I could still feel Val's fingers digging into my flesh as she pulled the tracker out.

"We don't think they have any way of tracing us," Jackson finished. "But we can't one hundred percent guarantee that. If you don't want us to stay, we get it. You need to protect your own."

"Fuck that!" Molly scoffed, her sweet eyes flashing with disbelief. She turned to Carl. "You better not even think about kicking them out because of me. And besides, this is *my* house. I get to decide."

"Baby." Carl tugged the beautiful blonde woman into his arms, lifting her chin with a knuckle. "I'm just tryin' to watch out for you. You know this life—"

She grabbed his hand, cutting off his words.

"Oh, I know, I know. It's dangerous. That's what I get for falling in love with you, but believe me, it's way too late to change that." She pressed a kiss to his lips then wrapped his arm around her waist, turning in his arms so she had her back pressed to his front. Her gaze took all of us in, landing on me last. Her face softened, showing both the sweetness and strength that lived inside her. "You'll stay until you're healed up, Alexis. And that's all there is to it."

CHAPTER EIGHT

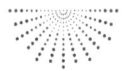

After all my years at Strand, I probably should've been the perfect patient. But maybe it was *because* I'd spent so long following doctors' orders and letting people fuss over me that I could hardly stand to do it now.

Molly was a great nurse, and she had four of the best, most willing assistants she could ask for—but her patient was a total pain in the ass.

Although my gunshot wound, broken arm, and bruised skull needed time to heal, I didn't want to give them that time. I wanted to be better already, damn it.

The first few days after I woke up in Molly's house, I didn't have the energy to do much of anything besides rest. But by the fifth day, I felt better enough to ask her to cut back on the pain meds. I didn't like how they messed with my system, making me feel groggy and a little out of it all the time. I was willing to accept some pain if it came with a clear head.

Unfortunately, once my mind became a little more alert, bed rest became nearly impossible. I was anxious and agitated, and no matter how well the guys took care of me, I wished I could take care of myself.

The topic of the mate bond seemed to have been silently declared off limits. I'd talked about it with Noah that first night after it happened, and the kiss we'd shared still played on an endless loop in my mind, but even he hadn't mentioned it since then. He hadn't kissed me again either, and I had a feeling they were all holding back because they didn't want to hurt me. Molly and Carl disappeared for long stretches at a time, leaving the five of us alone in her house. I was impatient as hell to get moving again, but the four men didn't seem to be in any hurry to leave. They threw themselves into my care wholeheartedly, following every one of Molly's instructions to the letter.

It was its own special kind of torture having them all so close, touching me tenderly to change my bandages, helping me get dressed, feeding and washing me—yet never going further than that. It was like they'd made some kind of pact among themselves not to take things further with me.

Shit. *Had they?*

I hated that idea. I would've hated it even before my wolf was called, but now that she'd risen and claimed each of them, I absolutely loathed it. Anytime I was around the guys, I had an undeniable impulse to get closer to them. There was physical desire—good Lord, was there ever—but it was more than that. It was like I ran on solar-powered batteries and their presence was the sun.

I couldn't help but think some of their enthusiasm for my care came from the fact that as long as they stayed focused on helping me heal, on tending to my needs, they didn't have to think about how completely and totally fucked we were. We had no plan left, no next steps laid out. The Lost Pack had scattered, and even though Val had given us the coordinates of their rendezvous point, I wasn't sure what good it would do to travel there.

Would we really go make a home in the wilderness and spend the rest of our days living in fear of discovery like the Lost Pack shifters did? What kind of life was that? How were they any less trapped now than they had been in the Strand complex's they'd escaped from?

Besides, our request for help from Alpha Elijah had already been denied, and I was sure the Strand ambush on his pack hadn't changed his mind. He'd refused point-blank to assist us in finding and rescuing Sariah.

Sariah.

The name scratched at my brain every time I thought about it. She kept appearing in my dreams—a young woman with dark hair and blue eyes like Rhys's. I'd never met her before in my life, but my imagination had formed a shape for her based on her brother's appearance, and I'd seen visions of her so often while I slept that I almost felt like I knew her already.

In my dreams, the two of us were trapped in the ambulance with the Strand hunters. And when I escaped, hauling my naked, broken body through the woods, I would turn back just as the ambulance exploded in a ball of scorching flame and realize that somehow, Sariah had been left behind.

I usually woke from those dreams sobbing and screaming, lashing out with such primal force that I tugged at my stitches and sent pain flaring up my arm. One of the men would pull me into his arms, where I'd cower, shaking and weeping, as the vivid agony of the dream faded.

Logically, I knew Sariah hadn't been in the ambulance with me. My memory of that day was patchy, confusing, and raw, but in all the flashes and snippets I remembered, I only ever saw four faces—three men and the woman who'd posed as my mother. Rhys's sister hadn't been in the vehicle. I was sure of it.

So why did she keep showing up in my dreams?

I would've been happy to forget the whole thing, to recall less and less of that awful day as time went by. But to my horror, the memories were sharpening instead, growing more distinct and clear. New snippets, sounds, and images assaulted me at random times, overwhelming me so completely I had to just close my eyes and breathe until they passed.

Maybe that was why I was such a bad patient to Molly. Laying still gave my brain too much time to work. Only forward movement could keep the past from catching up to me, so I did my best to keep moving forward—even at the expense of my healing.

That was exactly what I planned to do when I opened the door to the guest bedroom on my tenth day at Molly's house.

"No! Uh uh. Girl, you get back in bed right this minute." The sweet-faced nurse waggled her finger at me from down the hall.

It was still difficult for me to stand up completely straight, so I probably looked a little like Quasimodo trying to escape from the bell tower.

Damn it. Busted already, and I didn't even make it through the door.

"Rhys! West! Your little jailbird is escaping again," she called toward the kitchen. "Might wanna get her back in bed. I need to leave for work in a minute."

Double damn it. She'd called in my two bossiest caretakers.

West was still acting really strange around me and seemed physically incapable of looking me in the eyes right now, but that hadn't stopped him from taking care of me right along with the others. And for him and Rhys, that meant making absolutely sure I didn't break a single one of Molly's rules.

Sure enough, the sound of heavy footfalls followed her pronouncement, and a few seconds later, Rhys and West flanked her at the end of the hall.

So busted.

I dropped my head in defeat, still clinging tenaciously to the doorknob. The honest truth was, it was hard to stand without a little bit of assistance. But I was feeling better, and I was also on the verge of going crazy.

"Can I just come out for a little while?" I asked, peering

up to find Molly's face. "I just can't be in that room any longer. No offense! It's nice, I just…"

Pity washed over her features, and she nodded grudgingly. "All right, all right. If these guys will help you, you can walk around for a little bit. It'll be good to start getting your strength back. But don't go wandering around without help! If you push it, you'll only make your recovery take longer."

Relief flooded me, making my knees weak. Or maybe it was because I hadn't stood on my own for this long in days. I grimaced, tightening my grip on the door handle, and both men noticed it. In a flash, they were down the hall and at my side, holding onto my waist and my good arm to steady me.

Molly looked at the three of us, a curious expression crossing her face. She'd been watching us like that the whole time we'd been here, and I could practically feel the questions forming in her head about what exactly the deal was between me and these four men.

I was pretty sure the only reason she hadn't pressed for details was because it was so obvious to even a casual observer that the four horsemen, as she and Carl called them, cared for me and looked out for me. That they'd move heaven and earth to keep anything bad from happening to me.

"Well, I'm off to work. Be good, and don't let her stay on her feet too long," she instructed.

The two men nodded, and she headed out.

"You shouldn't have gotten up on your own," Rhys said gruffly.

The two men towered over my diminutive 5'3" frame,

and with them supporting me, my legs hardly carried any of my weight. I wasn't even sure this counted as walking. Levitating, maybe.

"It was fine. You guys were busy."

"No, we weren't. We're never fucking busy."

For the first time, I heard the same desperate impatience in Rhys's voice that I felt. I'd grown used to it on our long journey to the Lost Pack—nothing had ever seemed to move fast enough for him, no forward progress had ever seemed like enough. And it never would until he got his sister back.

It was reassuring, in a way, to know that he was as anxious as I was to move on. But it also made guilt stab at my stomach. The only reason they weren't moving on already was because of me. Once again, I was the one holding them back.

Maybe Rhys guessed at my thoughts, because he added in a low voice, "There's nothing *to* do. We lost her trail, and I don't know where to pick it back up again."

The pain in his words made an answering pain settle in my own chest. "I'm sorry, Rhys."

"Not your fault," he said shortly.

I knew he meant it, but it didn't make me feel much better. Whether it was my fault or not, I wanted to fix this for him, to do something to patch up the years-old hole in his heart.

But I didn't know how.

I let the subject drop as they maneuvered awkwardly through the door and guided me slowly down the hall. When we reached the living room, Jackson and Noah looked up from where they were parked on the couch watching a cooking show. Their obsession with the Food Network was both baffling and endearing.

"Hey, look at you, walking around like a fuckin' champ!" Jackson crowed, his amber eyes gleaming with delight.

"Yeah, right. More like being carried around like a champ."

To prove my point, I lifted both feet off the floor. West's hold around my waist tightened, and Rhys supported my good arm, holding me up.

Jackson grinned. "Hey, that still makes you a champ as far as I'm concerned. You're like a superhero. You can fucking fly."

I grinned. Jackson could be as serious as the others when the situation called for it, but he didn't choose to live his life in that headspace. He was like the poster child for making the best of a shitty situation, and I kind of loved him for it.

"You look better." Noah's slightly lopsided smile made heat pool in my belly and warmth fill my chest. "How do you feel?"

I waggled my head back and forth. "Better."

"Come on." West spoke without looking down at me, something I was sadly becoming accustomed to. "Let's get you a couple laps around the house and then we'll sit you down."

He and Rhys helped me walk at a slow pace around the small single-story house, supporting me as we went. I had to keep reminding them to let me do some of the work—then a minute later their grips would tighten and I'd have to remind them all over again.

By the time we made it back to the living room, some kind of barbecue competition was on TV. Noah and Jackson cleared a space for me between them, and the other two deposited me gently onto the couch. I leaned back against the soft cushions, more tired from the exertion than I wanted to admit.

I'd have to make a point to keep doing that as often as Molly would let me. I wasn't used to feeling so physically weak, and I didn't like it. I knew now that I wasn't sick, that I never had been—but it was hard to wipe away ten years of worrying about my health just like that. I'd probably always carry some of that fear with me.

Rhys and West settled into chairs on either side of the couch, and we lapsed into a comfortable silence. The guys would occasionally comment on someone's knife skills or cooking technique, making me wonder if they were all secretly master chefs or something.

My mind wandered as I watched the show through half-lidded eyes, the heaviness of sleep tugging at me. On the screen, a man was cutting up a large piece of meat. It was thick and red, and little rivulets of pink spread across the white surface of his cutting board like bloody cracks.

Acid churned in my stomach, a burst of adrenaline inexplicably shooting through me. My heart picked up speed, and I swallowed.

The man on the show picked up the pieces to dump them in a bowl, red drops spilling out from between his fingers. He grabbed another large slab of red muscle, and I clenched my jaw, trying to keep my stomach from revolting.

Red.

So much red.

It was everywhere.

In my fur. In my mouth. Spattering the inside of the ambulance like some sick Pollock painting.

It poured from my wounds, the fresh red blood mixing with the pools that had gathered underneath the dead bodies, already turning thick and almost black.

My hand reached out. No longer a massive paw, just a small human hand that shook with pain and shock. My palm and fingers were soaked in blood, and they slipped over the sheafs of paper leaving long, wet streaks in their wake.

As if I were finger-painting with my own blood, I left trails across the names printed neatly on the page, searching for one.

One name.

Sariah.

Patient #298. Salt Lake City, Utah.

"Alexis?" Jackson's concerned voice sounded like it came from a mile away. "You okay?"

I blinked, staring at the bloody meat being hacked up on the screen as my stomach churned violently. I squeezed my eyes shut, sucking in a breath as I let the memory wash over me again and again.

It was true.

It was right there. I wasn't imagining it.

"Shit. Turn it off, turn it off!" Noah cursed again under

his breath as the sound from the TV suddenly cut out. Then he put a gentle hand on my knee. "Fuck, I'm sorry, Scrubs. I didn't even think. It's over now. No more blood."

"It's... not that," I choked out, finally forcing my eyes open to gaze at the concerned faces around me. Horror overwhelmed me as more vivid memories of the fight in the ambulance filtered through my mind, but a fierce hope rose up in me too.

"Then what's wrong?"

I licked my lips. "It's... Sariah. I remember. I know where she is."

CHAPTER NINE

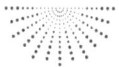

Absolute silence stole over the room, so complete I knew everyone had stopped breathing.

"What do you mean, Scrubs?" West asked carefully. "How do you know that?"

"In the ambulance, I saw a... a roster of some kind. Like a spreadsheet of the Strand test subjects. Sariah was on it." I dug my fingers into the soft cushions of the couch, fighting to sort through the new memories. "That's why I kept having dreams that she was there. Only, it wasn't *her* in the ambulance—it was just her name. That's what my dreams were trying to tell me."

"Holy fuck," Noah murmured, sliding a hand through his tousled blond hair.

"She's in a facility in Salt Lake City," I said, my voice gaining confidence.

I couldn't believe my mind had let such an important detail slip through the cracks, although so much of that awful event had been repressed by trauma and shock. But Sariah's name, her location—I was sure those memories were real. The images became stronger and stronger each time they cycled through my mind's eye.

Unbidden, my gaze shifted to Rhys. He sat straight and stiff in the large easy chair, barely breathing, his face frozen in an unreadable mask.

He blinked, rousing himself. His burning blue eyes met mine, and I saw a dozen emotions filter through them.

Then his expression cracked, like a piece of ice breaking apart on a hot day. A rough, inarticulate sound tore from his throat as he rose, reaching the couch where I sat in two long strides. He dropped to his knees in front of me and buried his face in my lap, his fingers digging into my hips. I could feel his body shaking with silent sobs, and I ran my fingers through his black curls, tears streaming down my own cheeks.

He stayed like that, kneeling before me like I was his queen, his idol, his salvation, as emotions that had been pent up inside him for days—weeks, *years*—finally escaped. His pack mates watched us solemnly as I whispered soothing words to Rhys, stroking his hair and running my hands over his shaking shoulders.

"I'll help you get her back, Rhys. We all will."

"Always, brother," West promised, his voice thick.

Noah and Jackson nodded, but I was sure Rhys didn't need to hear them speak to know they were with him too. We were all in this together.

A pack.

A family.

Finally, Rhys lifted his head from my lap, his sky-blue eyes lit with a fire I'd never seen in them before. He grabbed both my hands, devouring me with his gaze as he kissed my knuckles, his lips firm and wet from his tears. Each kiss he pressed to my skin was like a stamp, a promise. When he released my shaking fingers and cupped my face with his rough palms, the air suspended in my lungs.

Still gazing at me like he could never get enough, he brought his face close to mine. His breath wafted over my cheek, my nose, my lips, already claiming a part of me.

And then he kissed me.

In front of all his pack mates, as if he didn't give a flying fuck whether they saw, as if he'd die if he didn't, he kissed me.

His lips moved over mine, their touch so perfect and familiar already, although we'd only done this once before. But this was different than our previous kiss. The last time he'd pressed his lips to mine, he'd been taking something, claiming something.

In this kiss, he gave himself to me.

I took everything he offered, giving back as good as I got. The fear and nausea that had assaulted me moments before faded away, as though Rhys was my anchor, my shield from all the horrors in the world. As long as our lips were connected like this, our breath mingling and our hands twined in each other's hair, nothing could hurt me.

When Rhys finally pulled back, we were both gasping for breath.

"Holy shit." Jackson whistled from beside us. "That was hot."

A laugh bubbled out of my mouth as my head spun. Rhys's gaze met mine again, and the tears were gone from his mesmerizing blue eyes. In their place was adoration, devotion, and determination.

"Thank you, Alexis," he whispered roughly. His thumbs swiped over my cheeks, brushing away the tears I hadn't even known were still falling. "Fucking thank you."

He pressed his lips to my forehead, holding them there for a moment. I had a feeling he didn't want to stop touching me, and I certainly didn't want him to. I could happily live in this space for the rest of my life, surrounded by my four bonded mates, sandwiched between Jackson and Noah while Rhys worshipped me with his body and soul.

I bit my lip when he leaned back. "Of course, Rhys. I wish I'd remembered it sooner. But don't thank me yet. I just know what city she's in. I don't know where the facility is, I definitely don't know how we're going to get her out."

"We'll figure that part out. But knowing where she is makes it fucking possible." He rose to his feet, a manic energy growing inside him as he did. I could feel it radiating out from him, as though the very atoms of his body had started moving faster. He shifted his gaze to the other men in the room. "We need to move soon. Find out where the complex is. Figure out a better plan for getting in and out. Gather weapons, gear—"

"Woah, woah!" Noah put his hands up in a T shape. "Hang on a second. We can't go right now."

"We have to! There's no fucking time! We can't wait. What if they move her again? What if—"

The blond shifter stood, standing in front of Rhys to stop his wild pacing. "I know. You don't want to lose her again. I get that, Rhys, I do. We can start doing recon and making a plan right away. But we can't go anywhere until Scrubs is in better shape. She still needs to heal—she can barely walk."

"And I want to help," I insisted.

I meant it. I wanted to be a part of this. Not just because it meant something to Rhys, but because I was determined not to be the weak link in the team anymore.

Still, a small part of me wondered if the guys would even want my help. I didn't have nearly the same weapons or combat training they did, and although my wolf had single-handedly taken on four people in a speeding vehicle, she was also a total wildcard. I hadn't meant to shift and had barely been able to shift back.

Rhys's expression hardened, his fear at missing his last chance to save Sariah making anger rise in his features. His lips pulled back in a snarl, and he shook his head, shooting a glance my way.

I braced myself for what I had seen in his face so many times before: resentment and anger, frustration that I was holding them back.

But instead, the hard lines of his face softened when his gaze fell on me. He took a deep breath and blew it out, closing his eyes for a moment. When he opened them again, they were a little calmer. His clenched fists uncurled, and he slipped his hands into his pockets, dipping his chin in a small nod as he turned back to Noah.

"You're right. We need to take care of Alexis. We'll start planning now and be ready to go as soon as we know she's okay."

Warmth exploded in my chest, making it ache in the best way possible. I knew Rhys was one hundred percent devoted to those he loved. I'd seen it in him since the first day I met him, and even when the grumpy fucker had driven me up the wall, I had always loved how much he cared about the people in his inner circle.

And what he'd just told me, in not so many words, was that I was now a part of that circle. He would do whatever he could, even putting aside his own goals and plans, to make sure I was taken care of.

I tugged my bottom lip into my mouth, feeling new tears run down my face as I processed the enormity of that.

But worry niggled at my heart too, like a sharp spike driven into a tire, deflating my joy slightly.

If he lost Sariah again because we waited too long to act, I would never forgive myself.

Please, Sariah. Please be okay. We're coming.

IF I'D BEEN antsy and impatient with my healing before, now that I knew all the men were waiting on me to go after Sariah, I was a positive wreck. The next several weeks were a constant battle between always wanting to do more and having to hold myself in check so I didn't push too hard and set back the healing process.

Rest and time.

Molly reminded me over and over that those were the two things required for a complete recovery. That it was non-negotiable.

But we didn't *have* time.

And the more I thought about how little time we had, the harder it was for me to rest.

The guys continued to be the best nurses I could've asked for, but the ban they'd instituted on taking things further physically seemed to still be in effect—not counting Rhys's soul-stealing kiss. And although I knew it was probably for the best, my wolf didn't seem to give a shit about that. Every time I was around any of the men, I could practically feel her scratching at the walls of my ribcage, whining for me to seal the connection with my four bond mates.

Despite her constant presence inside me, she didn't truly feel like a part of me. More like an unruly guest who had set up camp in my soul and refused to respond to any of my commands, requests, or cajoling.

It made me feel nervous. As if I wasn't truly a shifter—not the way the guys were. And I wasn't sure how I could help them in a fight if I wasn't able to shift on cue.

After two weeks, my stitches came out. And another month after that, Molly told me I was clear to get my cast off. She had a massive medical supply kit—she'd mentioned that she used her nurse training to treat friends of Carl's who were injured in the line of work, and apparently it happened often enough that she kept her supplies well stocked.

I sat propped up in the bed in the guest room as Molly used a small cutting tool to remove the cast. It made a loud buzzing noise that grated on my ears, and I closed my eyes, turning my head away.

The hard pieces finally fell away from my arm, and I peeked at the newly exposed limb. It looked pale and thin.

Molly set aside the cast and started taking my arm through the series of gentle stretches and movements. As she worked, she shot me a look out of the corner of her eye, curiosity burning in her gaze.

"Okay, I gotta ask. I've tried to be good and mind my own business, but what can I say? I'm a nosy bitch at heart. What's going on with you and the four horsemen?"

My muscles tensed involuntarily, and she almost lost her grip on my arm. I glanced at her, wishing I could push down the blood coloring my cheeks.

But I couldn't, of course, and it totally gave me away.

Her eyebrows shot up. "So I'm not crazy! You and... all four of them?"

I chewed on my lower lip. "It's—it's complicated."

She laughed, the sweet sound filling the quiet room. "You can say that again. Shit, I can barely handle one. *Four?*"

My flush deepened, and I looked away, examining the bedspread beneath me with a sudden intense interest. *Jesus.* She probably thought I was some kind of nymphomaniac when the honest truth was, I was still a fucking virgin.

A virgin who just happened to be part wolf and was mate bonded to four men.

But I couldn't tell her any of that. I couldn't explain any of this.

"Oh, hey." Her cool fingers tipped my chin to make me look at her. "I didn't mean to upset you, Alexis. I've had enough people judge my relationship, I'd never do that to someone else. Hell, half my friends stopped talking to me when I got serious with Carl. If my parents weren't already dead, they probably would've disowned me. No one from my old life thought he was right for me, or good for me, or *good enough* for me."

She laughed softly, sadness reflecting in her kind blue-green eyes, before continuing.

"But you know what? Love doesn't care. It doesn't care about *who* or *how many*. It just *is*. And when you love someone with your whole heart, and they love you back the same way... that makes you perfect for each other, no matter what anyone else thinks. Because you'd do anything for each other, and that makes you both better."

Tears pricked my eyes as I thought about the four pack mates I'd fallen in love with. What they'd already done for me, and what I would do for them without question or thought.

"I didn't see it coming," I admitted. "It happened slowly, and then all at once. But they mean more to me than anyone I've ever known."

"I'd say the feeling is certainly mutual." She smiled, tucking her hair behind her ears and resuming her manipulation of my arm. "I've known the four horsemen for years, and I've never seen any of them look at a woman the way they look at you."

"Really?"

She lifted an eyebrow. "One hundred percent." Then she sighed. "Sorry. I really shouldn't have pried. It's just, sometimes, being in a room with all five of you—good lord, the sexual tension is so thick you could slice it up and serve it on toast."

I blushed. Shit. We were that obvious?

"It's okay," I assured her, trying to keep my voice from squeaking. "You're not wrong about any of it. It's just new to me. I still don't know what I'm doing."

A chuckle fell from her lips as she pressed her palm to mine, exerting gentle pressure to make me push back. "Don't worry, you'll figure it out. I never would've chosen to love Carl—on paper, we make no sense. But I *do* love him. I love the fuck out of him, and now that I know what my life is like with him in it? I wouldn't go back and change a single damn thing, even if I could."

We lapsed into a comfortable silence, but her words played over and over in my head.

I hadn't planned on any of this. And if someone had given me a choice at the beginning, I probably would've said no to all of it. But now that I found myself here, mated to four men, I realized Molly was right.

Even if I could go back and change things, I wouldn't want to.

If I'd woken up that first day in her house, and my wolf

had mate bonded to just one of the guys, I would've been devastated. Because as complicated as things felt right now, the truth was, I didn't want to choose between them.

I *couldn't* choose.

Molly did a few more stretches on my arm, nodding in satisfaction. "This is looking great. Considering the severity of the break, you healed up insanely quickly. You're lucky."

Did that have something to do with my altered DNA? Did my shifter abilities speed up the healing process somehow? I wished I could ask her, but I didn't want to draw any more attention to my unnaturally fast recovery.

And as memories of how I'd sustained my injuries flashed through my head, I shivered. "Lucky? I don't know about that."

She arched a brow. "Well, lucky is relative. It was unlucky this happened to you at all, but given that it did, your recovery has been stellar."

"So I'll be good to go soon?" I asked hopefully.

Rhys had been amazingly patient over the past several weeks—on the outside, at least. But I could feel the tension radiating from him no matter how much he tried to hide it. The guys had spent every minute they weren't with me searching for information about the Strand complex in Salt Lake City, but so far, they hadn't found anything. The organization was so clandestine that there was no record of any such facility in Salt Lake.

"Yeah. Should be."

She massaged my arm gently, making the unused muscles tingle. It felt a little uncomfortable, and my limb prickled as if it'd been asleep. As she worked, she hummed softly under her breath. It was so quiet I almost didn't hear it at first, but the sound slowly filtered into my ears.

When it did, my heart skipped a beat.

I knew this tune. It was the same lullaby the woman pretending to be my mother had sung to me whenever I felt low. It was a popular song; I'd heard it once or twice in movies or TV shows.

But I'd never heard anyone but my mother sing it in person.

It was our song.

A flood of emotions washed over me as Molly's voice strengthened, growing a little louder.

Guilt. Regret. Anger.

My wolf howled in my mind, pacing and whining inside me like a wild thing. She sensed danger, a threat, but she didn't know where it was coming from.

Molly stood up from the bed, pulling on my arm to bring me with her. I tugged back, resisting the pull out of instinct.

No! I can't let her take me. I can't let her kill me.

Jumbled, terrified thoughts raced through my mind, my breath coming faster as reason abandoned me. My body began to shake, and I stared into Molly's wide eyes without really seeing her.

All I could see was my mother.

And red.

With a loud crack, my bones began to break, sending pain tearing through my body. Molly gasped and fell back as my muscles rippled under my skin, my terrified wolf forcing her way out. Fur sprouted all over me, and the world took on a strange appearance through my new eyes. Everything was in too-clear focus, the sights and sounds too intense.

I crouched on my haunches, my huge form dominating the bed as a warning growl fell from my throat.

The woman in front of me screamed.

The sound was pure shock and terror, and it pricked my ears and made my fur stand on end. I couldn't remember any longer if she was friend or foe, but I knew prey when I saw it.

Leaping off the bed, I prowled toward her, the low growl still rumbling through my body. She screamed again and threw herself backward, almost tripping in her haste before slamming into the wall and pressing her back up against it, as if she could somehow pass right through it.

"Molly? *Molly!*"

A man with slicked-back black hair burst into the room, panic in his voice. My mates followed him, stopping dead when they took in the scene before them.

"Oh shit," Jackson muttered.

"*What the fuck?*" The man's eyes went wide.

The woman's gaze darted to him. "Carl!"

"Jesus fucking christ!"

He started toward me, a fierce, protective look in his eyes.

Without even thinking, I swung around to face the new threat, my legs tensing as I prepared to lunge for his throat.

CHAPTER TEN

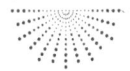

"Alexis, no!"

West's shout was a booming command, and I hesitated for a second, adrenaline and a predator's instincts urging me on. Urging me to attack. To strike first.

I bared my teeth again, but before I could strike, Noah and Jackson shifted. Their clothes ripped away from their bodies as they changed, and two large white wolves appeared, leaping forward to block my way.

Mine.

The recognition of my mates was even stronger in this form, and my wolf stilled, cocking her head to stare at them. Their presence comforted me, made it possible for the human side of my brain to rise to the surface and fight back the dominating presence of the wolf.

"What the ever-loving fuck?"

The man—Carl—tried to lunge forward again, but Rhys and West grabbed his arms, holding him back while Jackson and Noah approached me. Behind me, I could hear the woman—*Molly*—sucking in shaky breaths.

My wolf mates circled around me, nuzzling their noses into my fur, sniffing and huffing. I could smell them too, far better than I ever had in human form; their scents were comforting and distinctive, calming me further. My ears still twitched back and forth, searching for threats, but my hackles went down as the panic that had driven me to attack faded.

Jackson whined, licking my face. I was a full head taller than him in this form, a reversal that would've struck me as funny if I wasn't so terrified.

"Lexi." Rhys's gruff voice was steady, his bright blue eyes trained on me. "You need to shift back. Can you do that?"

My wolf tensed, hackles going up again. She didn't want to relinquish control.

"Fuck. She's too far gone." West shook his head. "We need to help her shift before she gets lost completely."

They both kept an iron grip on Carl's shoulders. The sharp-faced man had stopped yelling, but fear and distrust coated his features as his gaze darted between us.

"What... the hell... is going on?" Molly's words were halting and soft, and when I swung my head back to look at her, she sucked in a breath and pressed herself harder against the wall.

Like I was a monster.

A beast.

I growled, a sick feeling churning my stomach. The human side of me wrestled for control with my wolf, but it felt almost exactly like it would if we fought in real life. My wolf was huge and powerful, and I was small and puny; I could feel myself losing ground with each breath. I wasn't strong enough.

"Lexi. Look at Noah. Look into his eyes," Rhys said, as Noah's white wolf came stand in front of me.

His lupine eyes were the same soft gray-blue as they were when he was human, and the sight of them soothed me. Intelligence and kindness sparked in their depths, and I could feel the human looking out at me. I latched onto that, using his humanity to help me dredge up my own.

"That's good. That's very good. Stay with him. He's your mate, and he's here with you. We all are." Rhys kept talking, his deep voice pouring into my ears. "He's going to shift back. Follow him. Come with him."

"Come back to us, Scrubs," West whispered, so low I almost didn't hear him.

Keeping his gaze trained on mine, Noah began to shift back. I could sense Jackson doing the same, although I kept my eyes locked firmly on Noah, letting myself be drawn into his cloud-gray irises. His shape and visage changed as the shift worked its way through his body. I pushed to stay with him, allowing myself to feel the full force of the connection that existed between us.

Slowly, my body shifted along with his. It hurt like a fucking son of a bitch as my bones broke and reshaped themselves, and when I was completely human again, I fell to my knees, losing Noah's gaze as I gasped for breath. I finally started to understand why shifters didn't care about shifting back naked, because at that moment, my nudity was the last thing on my mind.

All I could think about was how much it hurt.

And how badly I had fucked up.

Noah crouched beside me, helping me to my feet as Jackson yanked the large comforter off the bed. They wrapped it around my body, ignoring their own nudity as they took care of me.

"What the fuck?" Carl had regained his voice, and it seemed like he'd keep asking that question until someone gave him an answer.

I had no words, though. What could I say to make him understand? To pick up the pieces of his mind and put them back together? To re-create the world he thought he knew?

So I turned toward Molly instead, guilt squeezing my heart like a vise. I'd almost attacked her. Because of an innocent tune she'd hummed—I'd almost let my wolf rip her throat out.

A memory of what that felt like, what it sounded and tasted like to kill someone that way, assaulted me, and I felt Noah and Jackson tighten their grips as my knees wobbled.

Molly stared at me with huge eyes, her face set in a mask of shock.

"I'm..." I swallowed. "I'm so sorry. I didn't mean to—"

I took a small step toward her, but before I could say anything else, Carl crossed the room in a few long strides, coming to stand protectively in front of his girlfriend. "Hey! Don't fucking touch her."

Tears stung my eyes. "I was just—"

His eyes narrowed dangerously. "Listen, sweetheart. I don't know what the fuck you are or what you're playing at. But you better get the hell out of this house right now."

"All right, man. All right." Jackson held out a hand placatingly, although the tension simmering in the air told me this situation was anything but *all right*.

Carl ran a hand over his slicked-back hair, facing us all down with a glare. Rhys and West grabbed my arms to support me while Jackson and Noah quickly grabbed new clothes. They pulled me out into the hallway, tugging on pants, shirts, and boots as we walked. When we reached the front door, West and Rhys pulled the comforter away from me and helped me slip into my own clothes. My hands shook so badly I could barely get them through the arm holes of my shirt.

I should've been happy I didn't have to navigate around a cast to get dressed anymore, but any happiness I'd felt about getting the cast removed had been entirely overshadowed by the events that'd followed.

Rhys tugged the hem of my shirt down, resting his hands on my hips to steady me. No one had spoken since we left the bedroom. I could hear the soft sounds of Molly and Carl's voices from inside the room, but I couldn't guess what they were saying.

"We gotta get out of here. At least long enough for him to cool off. If Scrubs shifts again, I don't know what he'll do."

"I won't—" I started, but broke off quickly. That wasn't a promise I could keep, and we all knew it. I hadn't meant to shift the last time, but it had happened anyway. And I could still feel my wolf pacing inside me, restless and anxious.

Jackson pushed the door open, and we stepped out into the midday sunlight. The air outside was hot and dry, and the sun felt good on my face; I'd gotten more used to the outdoors than I'd realized, and being trapped inside felt stifling now. Molly's house was in a quiet, unassuming neighborhood. The houses were small and old, but well-cared for. Palm trees and rock gardens graced the front yards.

Two strong hands grabbed mine, and I held onto them for dear life as Rhys and Noah supported me between them. We walked quickly down the street, leaving Molly's house behind.

"Well, fuck." Jackson's voice came from just behind me. His tone was light, but I could hear the weight of worry underneath it.

"I'm sorry," I whispered. My gaze flicked up to Rhys. "The first time we went to see Carl, you told me he didn't know. You said not to blow your cover. I didn't mean to. I'm so sorry."

"Don't worry about it, Lexi. It's not your fault." His jaw muscles twitched. "But I honestly don't know if we can go back there. I don't know what he's going to do."

"Carl wouldn't sell us out," Noah said, looking over my head at Rhys. "He lives by a code, and you know he actually means that shit."

"Yeah. But his code applies to humans. What if he decides *animals* aren't worth the same respect?"

The bitterness in Rhys's voice twisted a knife in my

heart. That was how Carl and Molly would probably see us. And try as I might to perceive things differently, it was hard not to see myself that way right now too.

West cleared his throat. "Well, we'll give him a while to calm down. But we have to go back and deal with it at some point. At the very least, we need to get our shit before we leave."

"What happened, Scrubs?" Noah squeezed my arm a little tighter, his soft blue eyes looking down at me.

"I... I don't know, exactly. We were talking. She took off my cast. Then she started humming a lullaby—a song that brought back old, awful memories. It freaked me out. I couldn't stop thinking about those people I killed, my mom trying to kill me. And my wolf reacted to my fear; I think she forced her way out to try to protect me."

"She's fucking huge. And beautiful." Awe sounded in Jackson's voice.

"She is?"

"Holy fuck, yeah. I've never seen another shifter like you."

My heart warmed at the tone of his voice, at the same time an icy chill washed down my spine. I hadn't been wrong. It hadn't just been my imagination. My wolf was different. And she was out of control.

We reached a small neighborhood park with a playground and some benches set up on a stretch of grass. Noah and Rhys steered me over to one, and I gratefully sank down onto the wooden bench. My legs were still shaky, and my body ached.

The others all gathered around. Jackson hopped up to sit on the back of the bench with his feet on the seat, sliding his fingers through my hair and massaging my neck.

"I don't understand," I said, forcing my eyes to stay focused. I wanted to retreat inside myself, where only the feeling of Jackson's strong fingers working out the knots in my muscles existed. But I couldn't. "What did Strand do to me to make me different? What does it mean?"

"We don't know, Scrubs," Noah said. "All we have are guesses. They were sneaky about dosing you too, pretending it was all to treat some mystery illness. In our case, they didn't bother hiding it at all. We got daily injections for a while, then less frequently, until our wolves finally came out."

"What did they inject you with? What does it do?" *What else is going to happen to me?*

"Not sure. Some of it was to force the change, to alter our DNA. And some of it was to keep the change from killing us... although it didn't work on all their subjects. I heard them refer to something called 'the source' a few times, but fuck if I know what that means."

"We can't say exactly what they did to you, because they were constantly experimenting. In our complex, they had different batches of test subjects," West said softly. "Some couldn't fully complete the shift. It was... ugly. None of them survived."

"No shifters have ever been able to get pregnant. And believe me, Strand tried." Rhys's voice held a hard edge, and West's nostrils flared. "Some people made the shift once and never shifted back. They kept those ones in a pen together, just in case it ever happened."

Noah must've seen the rising panic in my eyes, because he gestured to the others to stop. His hand fell on my knee, squeezing gently. "But you *have* shifted back, Scrubs. Twice. Your wolf is strong, and you'll have to figure out how to deal with that. But *you're* strong too. I know you can handle it."

I blinked hard, fighting back the tears that wanted to fall. His faith in me caused an ache in my heart, partly because I couldn't find any of that same faith in myself.

"When I shifted back there, I—I didn't even know Carl and Molly's names," I forced out. "I saw everything through my wolf's eyes, and they were just a man and a woman. And they were threats. What if you guys hadn't come in when you did? I could've killed Molly!"

No one contradicted me, and even though my heart sank, I appreciated that they weren't lying to me, coddling me to make me feel better. I wasn't wrong, and we all knew it. If things had gone differently, Molly's guest room could've ended up painted in blood just like the inside of that ambulance.

The thought made tears spill down my cheeks, and I swiped the back of my hand across my eyes, despising my weakness.

"What if I had attacked one of you?" I whispered, my heart cracking open at the words.

"Did you want to?" Noah dipped his head to catch my gaze, his earnest gray-blue eyes searching for something in my expression.

I remembered staring into those eyes as we shifted together from wolf to human. Remembered the relief I'd felt at having all of my mates there with me.

"No," I admitted. "I didn't. She knew who you were. She recognized you. She lov—"

I broke off abruptly, not ready to say the word. My feelings were real, whether spoken or unspoken, but I didn't want to tell these men how much I cared about them while sitting on a park bench after almost murdering two humans. An admission like that deserved a better moment than this.

The guys let it slide, although I saw warmth flash in Noah's eyes.

"See?" His thumb made gentle circles on my thigh. "She *can* control her hunter's instinct. And she won't hurt people she cares about. You just need to teach her to care about all the people you do."

I snorted. "It's a short list. It should be pretty easy for her to learn."

A grin tilted one corner of his lips. "I'm serious, though. You need to make peace with your wolf, let her be part of your life, or she'll always be 'other.' Wild."

I nodded slowly, biting my bottom lip as I tried to pull myself back together. "I can try."

The truth was, that was exactly how she felt.

Other.

Wild.

She felt like an uncontrollable, monstrous part of me that brought only death and violence every time she surfaced.

How was I supposed to make peace with that?

CHAPTER ELEVEN

"We better go back. I don't want to push our luck with Carl, but I don't want to give him too much time to stew either."

At West's words, I lifted my head from the firm pillow of Rhys's stomach. Jackson peeked up at me from where his head rested on my stomach. Noah was sprawled on the ground next to us, his fingers tangled in mine. After the guys had calmed me down a little, we'd gravitated toward the comforting patch of shade underneath the largest tree in the park.

The adrenaline of shifting and the fear of what I'd almost done had left me exhausted. When Jackson plunked down in the grass by the tree, I'd happily followed suit, and before I knew it, we were all lying together in a pile of warm bodies and hard muscles. It felt nice, and for a the past hour, I'd been able to shut off the worries assaulting my brain.

But at the prospect of having to face Carl and Molly again, they returned with a vengeance.

"Are you sure?" I choked out.

"Yeah." West pursed his lips. He leaned against the base of the tree nearby, and it didn't escape my notice that he'd deliberately kept distance between us. "If we don't get back there and talk to him, I'm afraid he'll give up our location. I hope we can trust him more than that, but I don't want to give him the chance to rat us out."

Fuck. He *had* been furious. If Carl was pissed or scared enough, would he call the cops on us? Or someone worse?

Jackson picked up on the worry in my eyes as he stood and tugged me to my feet after him. He pressed a kiss to my hair, wrapping his strong arms around me. "Don't worry, Alexis. We've known Carl for years. I'm sure he never fucking thought he'd see us turn into wolves, but he trusts us. We'll talk to him."

I couldn't imagine what they could say that would make any of this acceptable, but I forced my feet to move as we all headed back toward the house at a fast walk. West was right, we needed to get back there. Beyond the concerns about Carl betraying us, the simple truth was, we owed him an explanation—and Molly too. They'd opened up their lives to us, giving us shelter and aid with no questions asked.

And if they had some questions now... well, I really couldn't blame them.

When we reached the small, single-story house that had been our home base for the past six weeks, nerves prickled up my spine. Carl stood outside, and he looked up as we approached. I couldn't read his expression from a distance, but I saw his posture change as soon as he caught sight of us. He stiffened, standing up straighter and somehow seeming to inflate his muscles like a puffer fish. How the hell did guys do that?

The four shifters at my side noticed too, and our pace slowed a little. Noah and Rhys closed ranks around me, while Jackson and West fell into step in front of us. As if they were creating a human shield to protect me.

My heart warmed at the realization at the same time my stomach pitched. If one of these men got hurt trying to defend me, I'd never forgive myself. Rhys had already taken a punch standing up for me in that bar, and I wasn't sure I could bear to watch something like that happen again.

"Wondered if you'd come back." Carl crossed his arms over his chest, eyeing us assessingly as we came to stand in front of him.

"Wondered if you'd let us," West shot back, his tone carefully neutral.

"You can get your things. Then go." The sharp-faced man jerked his chin toward me. "Your woman is fine. Well, she's healed up, anyway. We did what we could for her, but I can't be gettin' into whatever shit you've got going on." He shook his head, a worried expression pinching his face. "I've got my own problems to deal with."

My shoulders drooped with disappointment. He was kicking us out? I shouldn't be surprised, but given the guys' history with him, and how much he'd helped us already, part of me had held out hope for a better response. He'd seemed almost like a father figure to "the four horsemen," as he called them, despite the fact that he was only ten years older, max.

I could hear the same disappointment in West's voice when he replied.

"Sure. We understand." He hesitated. "And then what? Are you gonna send the cops after us?"

"Don't you mean animal control?" Carl's nostrils flared, and his temper seemed to be working its way back up. His gaze flicked to me again, and I was certain he was remembering the way I'd prowled toward Molly as a wolf, destruction in my gaze.

Rhys made a noise low in his throat, moving closer to me, but Jackson broke away from our group.

"I'll get our stuff. I'll be quick."

He slipped inside the house, and the four of us stood facing Carl in a tense, awkward standoff.

When Jackson opened the front door again two minutes later, I was impressed with how fast he'd managed to gather our things—until I realized he didn't have any of it.

The reason for that became obvious immediately as Molly flew out the door after him, prodding him in the back to make him go faster. She darted forward to stand between Carl and us, her blue-green eyes flashing.

"You're kicking them out?"

Carl smoothed his hair back, shaking his head. "No, baby. They're just leaving."

"Like hell they are!"

I blinked. *She doesn't want us to go?*

Carl looked like he wanted to shake some sense into

Molly, but instead, he settled for glaring around her at me. "She tried to fucking kill you, Mols! I'm not letting them stay here."

She reached out, resting her hands on his chest and stepping closer to him. "Am I dead, Carl?"

He shook his head sullenly. "No."

"Am I hurt?"

"That's not the fucking—"

"Am I?"

I could practically hear his teeth grinding together as he answered.

"No."

"Then they're not leaving."

"Baby—"

He opened his mouth to argue again, but Molly pressed a kiss to his lips before he could say anything. Then she turned to face us, wrapping his arms around her body as she did.

"What the hell are you?" Her voice was soft, and her eyes held fear but also a burning curiosity.

"We can tell you everything," West said. "But it's probably better we don't have this conversation outside."

Carl heaved a breath and rolled his eyes, though his muscles remained taut. "Fucking fuck. Well, lucky for you, my girlfriend is a motherfucking saint—who also happens to be mildly obsessed with unexplained phenomena and the supernatural."

Without explaining any further, he turned on his heel and walked up the steps to the house, tugging Molly along with him. The rest of us shared a glance then followed.

As soon as Noah closed the door behind us, Carl spoke, crossing his arms over his chest.

"Okay. Spill it. And it better be fucking good, considering you've lied to me the entire time I've known you."

I wondered if that fact upset him as much as the fact that his longtime friends were part wolf. Although most of his business was on the wrong side of the law, he seemed to live by a very strict personal moral code. And that code probably didn't include lying to people you cared about.

"What you saw Alexis, Noah, and Jackson do? We can all do that." Rhys tugged his curly black hair into a bunch at the back of his neck before releasing the strands again. "We were test subjects of the Strand Corporation, and they've been creating shifters—part wolf, part human—for years."

Carl's bright green eyes narrowed. "Strand? The biomedical company?"

"Yeah."

"Jesus fucking christ." The older man shook his head, his brows drawing together. "I'd tell you to quit joking if I hadn't just seen you do it with my own damn eyes."

"No joke," Rhys said flatly.

"So why the fuck did that one attack my girl?" He jerked his chin toward me again, refusing to look at me or even use my name.

"It was an accident. Her wolf got agitated. But we won't let it happen again."

Carl scoffed. "How're you gonna stop it?"

"They won't!" I blurted. "I will." Sucking in a deep breath, I turned to face Molly, who had been watching the whole exchange with an intent look. "I swear, Molly. I will never, *ever* let that happen again."

I meant it too. Maybe I shouldn't have promised something like that when my wolf was still so out of my control. But if it came down to it, I'd rather hurt myself than her, and I'd do whatever it took to keep my wolf from attacking.

She stared at me for a moment, and I gazed right back, trying to imprint everything about her into my mind. The soft honey color of her hair, the way her smile was both sweet and a little wicked, the kindness in her eyes that seemed to infuse her whole spirit.

She wasn't old enough to be my mother by a long shot, but I'd started to think of her almost as a big sister. So many of my relationships throughout my life had been based on lies and manipulation, and the way Molly had helped me—helped all of us—with no expectation of something in return made the broken, dead parts of my heart heal over a little.

"I'm so sorry," I whispered.

When she stepped forward, I almost jumped back. I hadn't been expecting it, and I didn't want Carl to think she was in any danger. But although the sharp-faced man still seemed angry and on edge, Molly's hands were steady when she took mine in hers, squeezing them gently.

"You don't have to be sorry. You didn't ask for any of this. And you don't have to leave until you're ready."

CHAPTER TWELVE

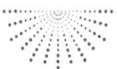

I stared at myself in the full-length mirror on the door of the guest bedroom.

It had been a few days since my accidental shift, and although Carl had grudgingly agreed not to kick us out, everyone in the house was walking on eggshells.

My hair, returned to its usual chocolate brown color, tumbled over my shoulders. Four wide, pink scars ran across my left arm, and my right arm looked pale and slightly thin. Although Molly seemed stunned at the speed of my recovery, I felt weaker than I would've liked.

Lifting the hem of my tank top, I ran my fingers over the puckered scar on the side of my abdomen. I knew if I turned around and peered over my shoulder, I'd see the scar between my shoulder blades where Val had dug out the tracking chip Strand had implanted under my skin.

I felt like a patchwork person, stitched together and sewn

back up, but somehow not quite the same as I had been before.

Would I be strong enough to fight with the men when they went in to rescue Sariah?

Would my wolf let me?

I could feel her inside me all the time now, growing more and more restless with each passing day. But I didn't know what she wanted from me. I had no idea how to reconcile the two parts of myself.

I leaned closer to the door, staring at the golden pools of my irises and the dark pupils that expanded and contracted as my gaze focused. I could almost see the wolf looking back at me through my eyes, feel her scratching at my ribcage.

The door opened suddenly, colliding with my face. I yelped and jumped back, bringing my hand up to my stinging nose.

"Oh fuck!" West's full lips pulled down in a grimace. "Sorry. I didn't mean to—"

"No, no. I'm okay."

I shook my head, trying to get my breath back. He'd startled me more than hurt me, and my heart slammed hard against my ribs.

West's strong hands cupped my face, his thumbs probing gently at my sore nose. It was the first time he'd touched me or even looked directly at me in days, and I stood perfectly still as he examined me, as if any sudden movement might scare him away.

"You'll be all right. It's not bleeding or broken."

His gaze caught on mine for a moment, and he seemed to

remember himself suddenly. He stepped back, scrubbing a hand over his short black hair. His dark skin was smooth, his lips full, and his features perfectly symmetrical. He even had dimples on both sides when he smiled, although I hadn't seen them much recently.

Not since my wolf had claimed him.

He cleared his throat awkwardly. "What were you doing?"

"Oh!" I blushed, dipping my head. "Just... looking. I wish I was stronger. I don't know how I'm going to get back to where I was before the accident. And I was miles behind you guys already. I just want to be able to pull my weight in a fight, you know?"

A strange look passed over his face, and he cocked his head. "Alexis, we found the guy in the woods you bit and crotch punched—he's the one who told us how to track down the vehicle they were transporting you in. I think you can hold your own in a fight just fine."

"Yeah, but that was just adrenaline and fear. I don't really have any training. And..."

I paused, wondering if I should put this on West. I knew he'd been avoiding me, and I didn't want to push him to talk to me if he wasn't ready.

But he tugged on my elbow, settling me on the bed before sitting down beside me. He still couldn't quite meet my eyes, but he glanced at me as he asked, "What's up?"

"Could you shift right now?" I asked, twining my fingers together. "If you wanted to?"

He cocked his head. "Yeah. Sure."

"I can't. And even if I did, I don't know if I could shift back. My wolf won't listen to me."

The admission fell from my mouth like a lead weight. I felt like a failure saying it out loud, and part of me was afraid he'd tell me that's exactly what I was. But instead, he sighed, leaning forward to rest his forearms on his muscled thighs.

"Sorry, Scrubs. I wish we could help you more."

"Can I do anything about it?"

He tilted his head to look at me before shifting his gaze back to the floor. "I don't know. The truth is, no two shifters are exactly alike. We're all experiments, given different doses of whatever the fuck serum did this to us. In the San Diego complex, Strand never stopped testing. They were constantly trying new things, manipulating us, making us..." He trailed off, his expression darkening. Then he shook his head, dropping whatever he'd been about to say. "Anyway, different people's bodies seem to react to the drugs differently. Some people never really make the transition work."

Fear gripped my heart like an icy hand. I was glad West didn't sugarcoat things for me, but his words made worry churn in my stomach. I'd hoped my problem was something all shifters went through, a natural part of the process. But how could it be when there was nothing *natural* about any of this?

"What does it feel like to you? Your wolf?" I asked.

He dropped his eyelids shut, like he was reaching deep inside himself, assessing what he found there. "It feels like the purest part of my soul. The part that knows exactly what it wants. That doesn't ask or worry or second-guess."

Since he couldn't see me, I was free to stare at him without making things horribly awkward, and I did, soaking up his even, dark features, wishing I could use my fingers to trace the lines of his face. He was so strong, so powerful, but there was a gentleness in him too. My body and heart craved both.

"That sounds nice," I murmured.

His dimples emerged as a smile tilted his lips at some private thought. "It is."

"So what does your wolf want?"

I was openly prying at this point, but this was the most West had talked to me in weeks. I wanted inside the seemingly impenetrable fortress of his heart and mind, and now that I saw a crack in the wall, I couldn't help but try to slip through.

His eyes popped open, catching me staring at him. I blinked, turning my head to look away, but his next words froze me in place.

"You, Alexis. It wants you."

The room seemed to shrink, as if the walls, the ceiling, and the very air around us were closing in, trying to force us closer together. I licked my suddenly dry lips, my whole body tingling.

"You—you have me. You're my mate."

West flinched at the word, the muscles at his temple rippling as his jaw clenched. His nostrils flared as his hand reached toward me with agonizing slowness, sliding through my hair to palm the back of my head. His pupils were dilated, and there was a wildness in his eyes as he seemed to fight some internal battle with himself.

"My *mate*."

The word was a rough growl, a curse.

But before I could process that, he pressed his lips to mine, wrapping his other arm around me to haul me onto his lap. My knees ended up on either side of his lean waist, my body pressed tight against him as he crushed me to his chest. This wasn't like the West who had kissed me back at the Lost Pack village. That West had seemed controlled, confident, unwilling to rush.

Now?

He kissed me like it was the last time he ever would, like an addict going back for one more fix before giving up their drug of choice for good.

I didn't know why. Didn't understand where this change had come from. But it hardly mattered when my body responded to his, lighting up like a spark under his touch. My breasts pressed against his chest, my nipples peaked and sensitive, and I felt the stiff bulge of his already hard cock between my legs. Our stupid clothes separated us, but I moved against him anyway, working my clit against his hardness, using the thick length to ease some of the intense, almost painful ache inside me.

He groaned, moving his hands to my ass to urge me on, pressing me harder to him as his tongue stroked against mine.

It felt like my wolf might tear out of my chest. The sounds of pleasure that escaped my lips were almost animalistic, soft grunts and whimpers that I hardly recognized as my own voice.

I needed this. I'd needed it since the moment I woke up on this damn bed and recognized all four men for what they were—my mates. But the circle was broken, the bond incomplete. And it would be until I became one with each of them, or at least as close to one as our physical bodies would allow. I needed to be connected to West, to feel him moving inside me.

Acting on instinct, I reached down between us, palming his thick cock through his pants. I squeezed it gently, making him buck his hips into my touch, then deftly moved my fingers up to work at his button and fly.

With a harsh growl, he stood, lifting me with him, and flipped me onto my back on the bed, crawling up to hover over me. I gasped in surprise before his mouth descended on mine, stealing all my breath. With courage born of desperate need, my hand moved down again, working its way inside his pants to feel the silky, firm heat of his cock against my palm.

When I stroked him, West moaned in satisfaction, delving his tongue into my mouth in the same rhythm as his hips pressed forward. My core throbbed with an aching need, and I released him for a moment so I could work the button of my own pants.

But before I could get them off, he suddenly tore his mouth from mine, rearing back to stare down at me with wide eyes. Then he scrambled away from me and off the bed, backing up until he was almost up against the door. His hands shook as he tucked himself away and zipped his pants back up.

He stared at me, chest heaving and dark skin ashen, as if he were looking at a ghost.

"West?" I rose up onto my knees, my heart still racing, my body still burning everywhere from his touch. I could feel the slickness that dampened my panties, but it was like a cold wind swept over me, chilling every part of me that had been warm. "What's wrong? I thought you said your wolf chose me. That you wanted—"

He shook his head, the movement jerky.

"Sometimes my wolf is wrong."

His hand groped behind him for the door, and before I could say another word, he wrenched it open and disappeared.

Confusion, frustration, and anger flooded in to fill the empty spaces in my heart his absence caused. In the suddenly quiet room, I collapsed back onto the bed, breathing hard. Then I rolled over, buried my face in the pillow, and screamed.

Damn the Strand Corporation and every one of their so-called 'doctors' for putting me through this.

Damn my wolf for wanting what she apparently couldn't have.

And damn these fucking infuriating men.

CHAPTER THIRTEEN

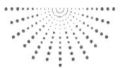

"Does it hurt?"

Molly's blue-green eyes cut to me curiously over the rack of clothes as she asked the question.

I blinked in surprise, but it didn't take me long to figure out what she was referring to.

The shift.

"Oh." I nodded, hefting my shopping bag higher on my arm. "Um, yeah. It does. A lot, actually."

"What does it feel like?" she pressed, lowering her voice to a whisper so the girl at the front counter of the clothes boutique wouldn't overhear.

"It feels like all my bones are breaking at once, and like my insides are stretching my skin. It's awful, but as soon as the shift is done, the pain goes away."

She nodded, chewing on her lower lip as she drank in my words.

Carl hadn't been kidding about Molly's obsession with

weird or unexplained phenomena. Once she got over her initial shock and fear, she'd seemed more intrigued by me and the guys than afraid of us. Which was good, since Carl himself still seemed to teeter on a knife's edge between accepting our presence and calling up Strand to report us himself.

I was still healing, but now that my cast was off, we had no reason to stay in Las Vegas—except that we still didn't know where to go when we left. Sariah was being held in Salt Lake City, but none of the guys had been able to find a more specific location than that. It was possible we'd have more luck when we got there and could conduct our search in person, but even that prospect sounded like digging for a needle in a haystack.

Regardless, my mates wanted a few more days to keep an eye on Carl, to make sure he wouldn't betray us the second we left.

Molly was the only one in the house who didn't seem affected by my attack and the revelation that we were shifters. Carl watched us with angry suspicion in his eyes, my mates were all on edge, and I felt like there were live snakes in my stomach all the time. But Molly seemed to think we could all go back to how it'd been before that awful day.

Today, Carl was at the pawn shop and my four mates were working on tracking down possible leads on the Strand location in Salt Lake City. Molly had seen me hovering anxiously over their shoulders and insisted on taking me out shopping. No one in the house had thought that was a good idea, me least of all; but I hadn't wanted to disappoint her after everything she'd done for me.

And to my complete surprise, I was actually enjoying myself.

This was my first girls' shopping day ever, and it felt good to do something normal for once—even if that normalcy was just an illusion.

Molly had taken me to a string of shops near the Strip, enthusiastically making me try on an array of outfits. I'd held off on buying too much, although I did indulge in a few things. I had no idea what kind of clothes I'd need once we headed out on our rescue mission, but I sincerely doubted that cute sundresses and strappy sandals would be necessary.

I'd also bought some lacy underwear and bras at Molly's insistence. She had beamed with delight as she declared that the guys would love them, and I'd turned red as a tomato and kept my head down as the clerk rang them up.

The small bag with my purchases hung off one arm as I flipped through the clothes on the rack. My stomach let out a loud growl, and Molly's eyes widened.

"Hungry?" she teased.

"Yeah." We'd been shopping for a few hours, and I'd never expected it to take so much stamina.

"We can grab a bite before we head home. There's a new Thai place I've been dying to try."

As we stepped out of the shop, I turned to face her, lifting a hand to shield my eyes from the midday sun. "Hey, Molly. I don't know if I ever said this, but—thank you."

She paused mid-step, then gave me a gentle smile. "Of course, sweetie."

After the truth came out, I hadn't seen any reason to hold back, so I'd told her everything. She knew about my isolated upbringing at Strand, about the woman who'd posed as my mother, and about my rescue from the complex outside Austin. I was pretty sure that knowledge had something to do with her insistence on taking me out today.

She knew how much of life I'd missed out on.

"I can't believe how okay you are with everything," I admitted, falling into step beside her. "Do you think Carl will ever get over it? I'm pretty sure he hates us all."

"He doesn't hate you." She shook her honey-colored locks as she led me down a smaller side street lined with a few boutiques and cafes. "Carl just doesn't trust easily. And he trusted the four horsemen. It'll take him a while to…"

She kept talking, but I lost track of her words as something caught my eye. A man had been leaning casually against the white facade of a building, but as soon as we walked by, he pressed away from the wall, falling into step behind us.

My heart picked up in my chest, slamming with dull thuds against my ribcage.

Don't freak out, Alexis. Maybe it's nothing.

My time on the run with the guys had made me paranoid and suspicious of every little thing. But with good reason—because even if the tracking chip inside me was gone, we were still being hunted.

Had Carl decided he didn't want to deal with us

anymore? That he didn't want to risk my wolf emerging again and hurting Molly? Had he turned us in to Strand?

I turned my head slightly, peeking at the man behind us out of the corner of my eye. It wasn't the blond Terminator, Nils, thank God. I didn't recognize the guy, but that didn't really mean anything. Strand probably had dozens—if not hundreds—of hunters I'd never seen.

But he was big, and everything about him felt like trouble. He was dressed casually in jeans and a dark t-shirt, but something about his bearing and the deliberateness of his walk made my skin chill.

He was following us. I was sure of it.

I looked back at Molly, who continued to talk, unaware of the danger stalking behind us. Trying to keep my fear from showing in my movements, I reached up and grabbed her elbow—hard. She jerked, trailing off as she looked down at me.

"Molly," I whispered. "There's a guy behind us. He's—"

But before I could finish the sentence, strong arms grabbed me from behind. I shrieked, struggling against the tight hold.

Another man I hadn't noticed leapt forward and wrapped his arms around Molly just as a large black SUV pulled up alongside us. The doors opened, and before I could even think about fighting against the iron grip wrapped around me, we were both picked up and shoved inside.

Our attackers leapt in after us, and a deep male voice yelled, "Go, go, go!"

The car peeled out, and I slid across the seat I'd been

unceremoniously dumped onto. The burly man who'd grabbed me yanked my wrists forward, binding them tight with a coarse rope. From the seat behind me, Molly screamed.

My pulse pounded in my ears, panic and adrenaline stealing all rational thought. I kicked as hard as I could, bucking my body off the seat as I lashed out. The man beside me grunted in pain as I caught him in the ribs, but the angle wasn't good enough to do any real damage. Cursing, he gathered my feet up, wrapping rope around them too.

"You got her?" the lanky guy in the driver's seat asked.

"Yeah." The voice came from the back seat, where I could still hear Molly grunting and jerking. She didn't scream again, and I wondered if they had gagged her.

The driver peered back over his shoulder. His cheeks were gaunt, and he had tattoos running up his neck to his jawline. His gaze fell on me, and he grimaced.

"Who the hell is that?"

"A friend of hers." The man sitting next to me shoved my feet away from him, forcing me to curl up into a ball.

"A *friend*?" The driver scoffed in disbelief. "Did I tell you to just fuckin' pick up anybody? The point is to teach Carl Lutsen a lesson. We got his girl. What the fuck do we need another one for?"

"I didn't want her callin' the cops. We'll deal with her too, don't worry about it."

"Jesus Christ." Neck Tattoo shook his head in disgust.

My mind reeled, trying to process everything that was happening. *Carl's girl.* She was the one they wanted, not me.

These guys were after Molly, and I'd just been picked up as collateral damage in her abduction.

Which meant Carl hadn't betrayed us—hadn't ratted us out to Strand.

But it didn't mean we were in any less danger. More, maybe, since I was pretty sure Strand wanted me caught alive if possible.

My breath came in short gasps as the SUV swung wildly around corners, shoving me up against the door and nearly tossing me off the seat onto the floor. Fuck. Where was a traffic cop when we needed one?

The wolf inside me whined, angry and afraid. I reached for her, trying to force the shift, but she slipped away, sinking back deeper inside me.

Damn it, damn it, damn it!

Noah hadn't been wrong. I wasn't treating her as a part of myself, but as an entirely separate entity. But I didn't know how to bridge that gap.

I struggled uselessly as we barreled down the streets of Vegas. Before I had a chance to formulate any kind of plan, the car screeched to a stop. The large, shaggy-haired man who'd grabbed me opened the door then wrapped his hands around my waist, hefting me easily from the seat. He threw me over his shoulder, knocking the wind out of me as his large deltoid slammed into my solar plexus.

Coughing and choking, I tried to lift my head. Behind us, I caught a glimpse of Molly's attacker dragging her from the car. The bag of clothes I'd been carrying tumbled out onto the curb as she struggled against the man.

"Ah, fuck. Help me! And grab that!" The guy jerked his chin toward my abandoned shopping bag, and the driver scooped it up.

Molly was taller than my diminutive 5'3" height, so the driver helped carry her as they followed us inside a rundown old house.

Every step Shaggy Hair took jostled me, making it hard to get my breath back. My arms and feet dangled uselessly, still wrapped tight in their binds.

The interior of the house was dark, and the whole place smelled of must and rot. Shaggy Hair dumped me on the floor unceremoniously, and sharp pain radiated from my tailbone. I rolled onto my side, trying to rise up to my feet, but he shoved me back down. Molly was tossed on the hardwood floor beside me, and for a moment, her wild, fearful eyes met mine.

What I saw in them scared the shit out of me.

She might not come from Carl's world, but she'd been around it long enough to know the rules of the game. And in her eyes, I saw the truth. We weren't getting out of here alive.

Teach Carl Lutsen a lesson. That's what the driver had said.

I didn't know what he'd done to piss these guys off, but the lesson they were going to teach him was that they could hurt him too. They could destroy what he cared about most.

We weren't hostages. We were going to be a message.

The three men gathered around to stare down at us, their booted feet leaving prints on the dusty floor.

"She's pretty." Neck Tattoo leered down at Molly before

turning his gaze on me. "So's her friend." He clapped Shaggy Hair on the back, chuckling. "Maybe you didn't fuck up so bad after all, bringing that one along. This'll be more fun if there's two of them to go around."

His words drove a spike of fear into my belly, and I renewed my struggles against the ropes binding me, sitting up halfway. "Let us go, you—"

Before I could make our situation worse by antagonizing our captors, Shaggy Hair lunged forward and backhanded me across the face. My head whipped to the side, and my body followed, collapsing in a heap on the floor.

"Mouth on that one." The third man snorted. "At least blondie here knows to keep her trap shut."

Molly's breath picked up, the harsh sound mingling in the dank room with my own. Groaning, I rolled over onto my back, searching inside me for my wolf. I could feel her distress, her confusion. Her anger.

Help me. Please.

Neck Tattoo cocked his head thoughtfully, his gaze flicking between me and Molly.

"You know," he said, to no one in particular, "Carl really shouldn't have such nice things. Doesn't that fucker realize it's just asking for someone to take them and ruin them?"

His tongue slid out, licking salaciously along his bottom lip. He pulled a butterfly knife from his belt, flipping it open with practiced ease. Then he crouched over Molly's body, chuckling as she went completely rigid.

"Scared?" His voice was soft, almost crooning. Like he really, really wanted to hear her say yes.

But despite her sweet nature, Molly was also tougher than almost anyone I'd met. She didn't give him the satisfaction, just watched him with wide eyes, nostrils flaring and jaw clenched.

Neck Tattoo smiled wider, seeming amused by her response. "It's okay. You will be."

He dragged the knife down her cheek, pressing just hard enough to leave a small red line in its wake. An involuntary noise of terror fell from her lips, and she squeezed her eyes shut.

I wanted to do the same, but I couldn't. I couldn't stop staring at the knife. The wickedly pointed tip, the dull light that glinted off the blade, the way the man held it so steady against her skin.

So many of my relationships for most of my life had been based on lies. After finding out how much I'd been manipulated by the people I trusted, I had wondered hopelessly whether I'd ever trust anyone again.

But I trusted Molly. What was more, I liked her.

I cared about her.

My wolf pawed at the inside of my ribcage, her distress—*my* distress—rising. These fuckers were going to hurt Molly. They were going to kill her.

A harsh yell tore from my throat, the sound morphing into a howl as I tipped my head back, my back arching off the floor. Every muscle in my body tensed, like a rubber band stretched to the breaking point.

And then it snapped.

CHAPTER FOURTEEN

My wolf rose to the surface, tearing her way out of my body as if she had to rend me to pieces to rebuild me whole. Bones broke under my skin, tissues growing and changing. The binds on my wrists and ankles snapped as the shift tore through my body like a hurricane.

The pain was just as intense, but the shift was over faster than ever before. I sprang to my feet, shaking off the last vestiges of pain as a full-throated growl rumbled in my wide chest.

"What the *fu*—"

Neck Tattoo didn't even get to finish speaking. I was on him in an instant, viciously and unrepentantly snapping my jaws around his neck. He gurgled, his body jerking once. I shook him for good measure, his blood coating my tongue as he went limp as a rag doll.

My ears pricked as shouts and curses from behind me called my attention. I released the lanky man and spun around, my keen wolf eyes taking in the room. Molly had scooted backward on her butt, her bound hands in front of her.

This time, the fear in her eyes didn't call out the predator in me.

It called out the protector.

This woman with the soft laugh and kind eyes was my friend, and I'd be goddamned if I let anyone hurt her.

I shifted my gaze away from her, my bloodlust rising again as I faced down the two men who'd intended to do just that. They stared at me in shock, too surprised to even reach for their weapons. As my gaze met Shaggy Hair's, he finally lurched into action, diving for the gun on the couch. I chased after him, teeth closing around his calf. The fabric of his pants tore, and when he went crashing to the floor, I sprang up to land on top of him, ending his life with the snap of my jaws.

The third man reached the gun, snatching it up and aiming at me with shaking hands. He squeezed the trigger just as Molly swung her bound feet toward him in a wide arc. She caught one of his legs, sweeping it out from under him. The gun went off as he went down, sending a bullet flying up into the ceiling.

Fury ran through my veins like hot metal, and I leapt on the man. My paws landed on his shoulders, pinning him down as I tore at his flesh until blood dripped down my muzzle.

When his struggles finally ceased, I drew back, tongue lolling out as I panted. Memories of my fight in the ambulance crowded my mind as I looked around at the three fallen men. Blood pooled around each of their bodies, and the smell of it hung like a tang in the air, overriding the scents of mold and dust. I whined, shaking my head. Little droplets of blood flew from my fur, peppering the dirt streaked floor.

Several drops landed on Molly, who'd worked her way up to her knees, her wrists and feet still bound. Her eyes were wide, as if she was realizing for the first time exactly how awful her first encounter with my wolf could've been.

I let out a whuff, lowering my head. The sharpened sights and sounds that assaulted me in this form pressed in around me, and I closed my eyes, panting heavily as I tried to force the shift back to human.

The floorboards creaked, and soft fingers stroked my fur. I lifted my head, eyes popping open. Molly had scooted closer, allowing her to reach out and touch me. I could still see fear reflected in her eyes, but she didn't pull away when I swung my head toward her.

She trusted me.

Warmth spread through my chest at the thought, bolstering my strength of will. With agonizing slowness, I cajoled my wolf into relinquishing control, and the shift finally rippled through my body, retracting my fur and changing my shape.

When the sharp pain finally receded, I found myself crouched on all fours on the floor, slick blood coating my mouth and face. The room felt cold now that I no longer had clothes or fur to cover me—or maybe it was just my body reacting to the shift. Goose bumps broke out across my skin, and I shivered uncontrollably as Molly helped me to my feet. She'd kept her hand on me the whole time I'd shifted, grounding me and lending me strength.

"Oh my God, Alexis. I can't believe—" She swallowed, wrapping an arm around me to help me stay upright. "You saved my life."

By ending three others. I didn't want to linger on that thought too long, so I just nodded, trying to making my knees stop wobbling.

"We need to get out of here," I said breathlessly.

"Right. Shit."

Her gaze flicked down to my naked form before she scanned the room. The place didn't look like it'd been lived in for a while. Besides the beat-up couch, there was a small table along one wall with a few empty beer cans on it, but not much else. My shopping bag lay on its side by the door.

The open butterfly knife had clattered across the floor when I attacked Neck Tattoo, and I stumbled over to it, then used it to cut through the binds around Molly's wrists. Her feet hadn't been tied like mine had.

"Thanks." She rubbed at the skin of her wrists, which was raw and red. "Here, let me help you."

She guided me across the room to where the men had carelessly dumped the bag of clothes that had fallen from the car. After pulling out a soft green sweater, she used it to help me clean the worst of the blood off my face, arms, and torso. Then she tossed the stained red garment aside and dragged another item from the bag—the sundress I'd bought.

"Here."

She bunched it up and pulled it over my head. The cheerful yellow color turned red in spots where blood still clung to my skin, and a wave of sadness washed over me. This wasn't what I had envisioned for this dress. Not by a long shot.

Molly darted over to grab my shoes—the only article of clothing that hadn't been destroyed by my shift—and I slipped them on. With one last look at the bodies sprawled on the floor, we rushed out of the house.

The neighborhood was quiet and rundown. Graffiti tags dotted the buildings, and no cars passed us on the street. My gaze darted from house to house, seeking out the next threat. The lack of activity was threatening rather than calming—this was a neighborhood where people came to do bad things without getting caught.

The soft fabric of my sundress flapped in the wind as Molly and I ran down the street. I had no idea where we were, so I followed her lead, sprinting flat out until we finally came to a larger street. Molly raised her hand and gave a piercing whistle, and a yellow cab pulled up to the curb.

"In. In!" She wrenched the door open, gesturing for me to go first. I slid inside, and she followed, blurting her address to the driver as she did.

The middle-aged man gave us a wary look, and I ducked my head, trying to hide the streaks of blood I was sure still coated my skin. When he put the car in gear and pulled back into traffic, I let out a shuddering breath.

Molly and I both turned to look out the back window. I

kept expecting to see the lanky, tattooed man or his shaggy haired friend come running down the street after us.

Except, they wouldn't.

They were dead.

There was no one left to chase us.

I tried to let that thought comfort me, but it only made nausea roil my stomach.

Three more people were dead because of me. In the space of less than five minutes, I'd ended three lives.

And the most terrifying part of all was that I really wasn't sorry about it. I could still feel the muscle and bone tearing and snapping between my teeth, could still taste the blood. And the part of me that was wild, that was all wolf, had relished it.

Molly didn't speak, but her hand slid across the seat, palm up. I grabbed it, squeezing tight, and we stayed like that the entire drive back to her house. She called Carl on the way, and although their conversation was brief, I could practically feel his tension radiating through the receiver.

She instructed the driver to stop several blocks away from her place, and we waited until he'd driven off before we walked the final distance. Just in case.

Her neighborhood was quiet in the peaceful way, but the friendly palm trees and nicely tended yards didn't seem to fit the chaotic mess of emotions churning inside me.

I staggered up the front steps behind Molly, my knees shaking. When she pushed open the door, the five men standing in her living room all looked up.

There was a moment where time seemed to suspend,

seconds drawing out into little slices of eternity. Four sets of eyes riveted to me, the emotions blazing behind them almost knocking me back a step. Then everyone moved at once.

Carl met Molly in three long strides, sweeping her into his arms and crushing her to his chest. And my wolf shifters converged on me, enfolding me in the warm cocoon of four massive bodies. Even West joined the pile, his nose pressing into my hair as he breathed deeply. I was showered with kisses, eight hands skating over my body as if to verify that I was really here and whole.

Finally, they unwound themselves from around me, pulling back to examine me and let me get some air. I'd barely been able to breathe in the tight hold of their embrace, but I missed it immediately.

West's awkward coldness returned as he stepped away from me. It somehow felt like every time he touched me, he had failed at something. Like he kept promising himself to never do it again.

Noah held onto my shoulders, his gaze skimming up and down my form, taking in the blood. "You shifted again?"

I nodded silently.

"What the hell happened? Who took you?" Carl looked down at Molly, a dangerous expression on his face. I'd never seen him look so angry, not even when he'd burst into the guest room and found my wolf threatening Molly.

She explained what had happened quickly, her voice low but steady. When she reached the part about me tearing into the three men, she spoke almost robotically, reporting the basic facts without giving any extra details. I wasn't sure if she was trying to protect me from Carl, or to protect Carl from me. Or maybe she just didn't want to relive it. I couldn't blame her.

When she finished, the murderous look on his face had only deepened. He shook his head. "Travis Sims. That fucking cock. He was convinced I was stealing business from him, but I wasn't. He was a slimy dirt ball—no one wanted to hire him twice."

Molly nodded, her bright gaze meeting his. I remembered our conversation about love and wondered if, in this moment, she regretted falling in love with Carl. If she wasn't part of his life, his world, she would've been safe today. It was their relationship that had put her—*us*—in danger.

But she answered that question for me when she rose up on her tiptoes and kissed him fiercely. He kissed her back, his hands clutching at her body like he was afraid she might evaporate any second. From the way all of my mates still had their hands on me, and the way they gathered around close, giving me only enough space to breathe, I guessed they felt the same way.

Carl finally broke the kiss, pulling Molly into his embrace again and meeting my gaze over her shoulder. His green eyes glittered intently as he dipped his head.

"Thank you, Alexis. I owe you."

CHAPTER FIFTEEN

Breathing deep, I gave Carl a small smile that probably looked about as sickly as I felt.

Noah hadn't stopped staring at me, concern filling his expression. "Are you all right, Scrubs?"

I nodded, although even that gesture made me feel a little woozy. The room seemed to keep moving in my periphery even after my head stopped, and I blinked hard.

"I'll help her get cleaned up."

Jackson wrapped an arm around my shoulders, which still prickled with goose bumps. I couldn't seem to get warm, even though the air outside had been hot and dry like always.

He guided me toward the bathroom, and I walked on numb legs. When we reached it, he perched me on the closed lid of the toilet and left, returning a moment later with a change of clothes.

"I got a long-sleeved shirt. It'll help you warm up." He

tugged me to my feet again, his usually laughing face serious as he gazed at me.

I caught a glimpse of my reflection in the full length mirror on the back of the closed door and blanched. I looked like a horror show. Despite Molly's attempts to help me clean up, my mouth and face were still stained with streaks of drying blood.

"Nice dress." Jackson grinned at me, a little of his usual spirit returning. "Is it new?"

A choked laugh bubbled up my throat. "I bought it today. You like it?"

"Yeah." He cocked his head, considering the bloodstained yellow dress. "It's like 'beachy badass.' Is that a thing?"

I laughed again. The sound was almost manic, but it felt good, as if it opened some kind of release valve on my pressurized emotions.

Jackson stepped around me to turn on the shower, tugging the curtain closed while he waited for the water to heat up. My legs still felt unsteady, so I sat down on the closed toilet again while I watched him test it with a hand under the spray. His focus and concentration were adorable. He was so earnest, so uninhibited. I never had to guess what Jackson was thinking or how he felt.

Unlike some of the other men in my life.

"Jackson?" I asked softly. "Is West mad at me? Does he not trust me anymore?"

He pulled his hand back, shaking the water droplets off as he turned to face me. "No way, Alexis. He's not mad at you. What makes you think that?"

I swallowed. I wasn't in a great emotional place to have this conversation, but I'd brought it up, so I forged ahead. "Ever since my wolf came out, he's been so weird. It's like he doesn't trust me—or himself around me. Is it because my wolf keeps losing control?"

He sighed, leaning against the wall near the shower and running a hand through his dark brown hair. "No. It's not that at all."

"Then what?" I pressed. "I always thought it was Rhys who hated me, but it's like he just passed the baton off to West."

A chuckle rumbled in Jackson's chest. "Man, they really are grumpy fuckers, aren't they?"

I almost smiled, but the nerves pitching in my stomach wouldn't let me. "Yeah. Sometimes."

He seemed to debate something internally for a moment. Then, having reached a decision, he crouched on the balls of his feet in front of me, resting his hands on my knees. His amber eyes sought mine, a haunted look in them.

"It's not you, Alexis. It's him. When we were at the San Diego complex, West was forced into a mate bond—the doctors were running some new 'experiment' or other, and decided to play God some more. They managed to force the connection, but it wasn't a true mate bond. It—it was super fucked up."

He shook his head, and the expression on his face made me sure that as horrible as what he'd just said sounded, I'd gotten the sugar-coated version.

"It messed him up bad," Jackson continued. "Even after

the docs scrapped the experiment, he wasn't the same for months. And now, what he has with you—what we *all* have with you... It's a real mate bond, I'm sure of it. But he doesn't trust it. He can't let himself accept it."

I bit my lip, wanting to cry at the pain in Jackson's voice, at the thought of West suffering like that. I hated that the bond between us was opening those old wounds, and as much as I needed West in my life, I wished there was some way I could release him from this. Free him from his torment.

Jackson must've read the look in my eyes, because he gave my knees a squeeze. "He'll come around, Alexis. I promise."

My chin jerked in a half-nod. It was all I could muster. The weight of the day was finally catching up to me, and I felt shaky and exhausted.

"Good," he said. "Let's get you clean, okay?"

He rubbed my legs where new goose bumps broke out, then pulled me gently to my feet. The water had heated up while we talked, and now puffs of steam filled the bathroom.

Jackson's hands skimmed up to the straps of my sundress, and he looked up, meeting my gaze. "Can I?"

I dipped my chin again, unable to look away from his beautiful eyes. With gentle care, he slipped the straps off my shoulders. The dress was loose and breezy, and without the straps holding it up, the fabric slid easily off my body, baring me completely. His gaze trailed downward, his attention warming my skin like beams of sunlight.

Then he reached a hand over his head, tugging off his own shirt before shucking his pants and shoes, leaving him in just a pair of black boxer briefs. He helped me into the tub then joined me, reaching around me to adjust the temperature slightly.

He positioned me under the spray of water before lathering his hands with soap. Little droplets clung to his broad pecs and shoulders, trailing down through the sprinkling of dark hair on his chest. When his hands began to massage my skin gently, working their way down from my face and neck, over the line of my collarbone, and across my shoulders, I let out a small sigh.

It felt like I was melting, becoming an entirely new form. As if his touch was changing something fundamental about the makeup of my being.

And I liked this version of me so much better.

My eyelids drooped as I lost myself in the wonderful feeling, letting him take control as the tension drained from my body. His touch was gentle, worshipful, and when my gaze dropped down, I saw that he was hard. A thick bulge pressed against the fabric of his wet boxer briefs, straining toward me. But he ignored it, even as his hands moved down over my breasts, letting pink, soapy water trail over my body as he washed the blood away.

My nipples peaked under his palms, and a dull, throbbing ache began to build in my core. I was as affected by his reaction to me I was by his determination to ignore it so he could take care of me.

This mate bond between us, whatever it was, was more than just attraction or lust. I'd never felt more sure of that than I did this moment.

It was love. Tenderness. Caring.

I bit my lip, overwhelmed by an onslaught of emotions. Unbidden, my hands reached out to touch him the same way he was touching me, sliding over the smooth skin of his arms, over his shoulders, and across his chest. His movements paused briefly, and his Adam's apple bobbed as he swallowed.

"Turn around," he commanded.

The two words were a rough whisper, and I could tell my touch was straining his self-control. But I didn't care. These men all had way too damn much self-control as far as I was concerned. They were my mates. I should be able to touch them, be close to them, if I wanted to. And the feel of Jackson's large hands on my body made me feel whole and alive.

I did as he ordered, turning my back to him and letting the spray of the shower pour over my chest and shoulders. He washed my hair, his thick fingers massaging my scalp. Then he urged me forward so the water ran down over my head, washing the suds away.

The bulge of his cock brushed against my low back, and when he moved to pull away, I moved with him, pressing my back to his front as I molded our bodies together. He let out a groan as I shifted against him, and his arms wrapped around me to strengthen the connection between us.

He dipped his head, ghosting his lips over my wet hair, across the shell of my ear. When they trailed over the line of my jaw, an explosion of sensations zapped through me like lightning. I squirmed in his grasp, turning my head to capture his mouth with mine.

Finally.

Perfection.

I had needed this for so long, and it was better than anything I'd imagined. Jackson kissed just like he lived, with open-hearted, passionate abandon. His lips moved against mine, his tongue darting out to caress the seam of my lips, and when I opened to him, he tasted me like a starving man. His hands slid up to cup my breasts, and I gasped into his mouth.

In a quick motion, Jackson broke our kiss and spun me around to face him, backing me up against the side wall of the shower. His big hands framed my face as he looked down at me, his cock pressing into my belly.

"Fuck, Alexis. I really didn't mean to start anything."

"I know," I whispered breathlessly. "I think *I* started it."

He chuckled. "Yeah, maybe you did." He dipped his head to kiss me again, making the world spin as his mouth explored mine.

When we broke apart this time, I grabbed onto his strong shoulders to steady myself. If I'd felt shaky when we first stepped into the shower, my knees were like Jell-O now.

But this kind of shaky, I didn't mind. In fact, I wanted more of it.

I rose up on tiptoes to kiss him again just as a knock came at the door.

It scared the crap out of me, bursting the little bubble we'd created where nothing existed but quiet groans and hot steam and our warm bodies. I jumped, and I probably would've slipped and cracked my head open if Jackson hadn't steadied me with a strong grip.

His brows furrowed as he raised his voice to call out, "Yeah? We're a little busy in here!"

I half expected it to be one of his pack mates teasing us about taking too long. But when West's voice came through the door, there was nothing teasing in his tone. His voice was curt and hard with worry.

"You better get out here. You need to see this."

CHAPTER SIXTEEN

Jackson's eyes met mine, worry darkening their amber glow.

"Okay!" he called. "We'll be right there!"

He must've heard the same thing in West's voice I had, because he didn't waste any time. The perfect bubble between us burst completely when he reached over and turned the knob, shutting the water off. He helped me out of the tub, handing me a fresh towel before wrapping one around his own waist.

Then he pressed a kiss to my hair, heat returning to his gaze for just a second before he whispered, "Are you okay to get dressed on your own? I'll throw on dry clothes and meet you out there."

I nodded, nerves already rising up inside me as he slipped out the door.

What was wrong now? Had Strand found us? Had the

bodies of our abductors been discovered? Were more of Carl's enemies after him?

The more time I had to think, the more horrible scenarios I dreamed up. So I dressed as quickly as I could in the jeans and long-sleeved shirt Jackson had brought me. He'd delivered shoes too, but I didn't even bother putting them on, just grabbed them and carried them down the hall to the living room.

Voices greeted me, but no one in the room was talking. The only sound came from the TV, where a CNN news anchor addressed the camera.

"—that Terrence Cole, the CEO of the Strand Corporation, has died unexpectedly at the age of fifty-four. Doctor Alan Shepherd, Cole's right hand man and long-time partner, will be taking over as head of the company."

To the left of the perfectly manicured announcer, an image appeared of a middle-aged man with short brown hair and blue eyes.

I blinked, all the air escaping my lungs in a rush.

Doctor Shepherd.

The man who had been my caretaker, mentor, and friend for almost half my life.

The man who had utterly betrayed me. Lied to me. Used my fears and hopes to keep me pliable as he performed unconscionable experiments on me.

My legs went weak, my shock at coming face-to-face with him making me dizzy—never mind that he wasn't really here, was probably hundreds of miles away.

Strong arms wrapped around me from behind,

steadying me before I collapsed. Jackson had just entered the room after me, and he gave me a gentle, reassuring squeeze before we both turned our attention back to the television.

"It's unclear what this will mean for the future of Strand. The company is notoriously tightlipped about its operations and has come under criticism for refusing to disclose all of its business dealings."

"That's right, Stacy. But given Doctor Shepherd's presence at Strand since the company's inception, it seems unlikely the direction of the company will change drastically with him at the helm," her co-anchor put in, turning to her with a serious expression. "Shepherd, who's remained out of the public eye for the most part, preferring to leave the media attention to Cole, issued only a brief statement in response to the news of Cole's death."

She nodded, picking up the story with practiced ease. "He said that he would honor the vision Cole had for the company and mentioned that they would be ramping up spending on research and development, making that the Strand Corporation's main priority in coming years."

The newscasters continued talking, passing the story back and forth like two kids tossing a ball at recess. But I stopped listening.

More research and development.

These perfectly polished news anchors might not know what that meant, but I did.

More human experiments.

More lives stolen.

And who knew what would happen to the ones they already had.

"—has been criticized for its ties to overseas dictators. Some speculate that Strand has been trying to produce biological weapons, although no evidence of any such wrongdoing exists," the female anchor said, her blandly pleasant voice drawing my attention once more.

"Yes. Given those allegations, it'll be interesting to see whether Shepherd chooses to be more transparent about the company's dealings, or if he'll follow the precedent established by Cole."

The image on the screen shifted, and the two anchors moved on to other breaking news, speaking in the exact same cadence and rhythm, as if all their stories were essentially the same.

I was finally able to pull my focus from the TV set, and my gaze flicked around the room. Noah and Rhys sat in the two large chairs on either side of the room while Carl and Molly shared the couch, and West stood near the hallway entrance where Jackson and I hovered.

Wordlessly, Carl snatched up the remote from the cushion beside him, pressing a button to mute the TV. The newscasters' mouths continued to move, their expressions neutral but serious, as text scrolled across the bottom of the screen.

The room fell into a thick silence, broken only by the squeak of the chair spring as Rhys's feet bounced in agitation.

"Motherfucker." West's voice was a low growl, full of

more hatred than I'd ever heard in my life. "*More* research and development? Hasn't he made enough of us by now?"

"And I'd bet every damn thing I own he'll try to sell the new models as weapons," Jackson said in a disgusted tone, his chest vibrating against my back. "Did you catch that bit about their ties with overseas dictators?"

"Yeah. I caught it. We—"

"We have to go. Now!" Rhys exploded up from his chair so fast I jumped in surprise, shrinking back into Jackson's embrace. The black-haired shifter ran a hand through his long hair as he paced across the room, eyes flashing. "Right now! Let's go!"

He moved toward the hallway, apparently intending to grab our stuff and walk out the door this minute, never mind that we had no means of transportation and no solid idea where we were going.

West stepped into his path, putting a hand on his chest. "Woah, slow down, man. You're right, this is bad. And you're right that we can't wait any longer. Alexis is doing better, and if we don't get to Sariah soon, who knows what kind of shit they'll try to do to her. But we need a plan."

"Fuck a plan! We've spent weeks digging for information on a Strand location in Salt Lake, and we've found shit. We're not getting anywhere trying to do this from a distance. We need to. *Be. There*. I'll knock down every fucking door in the city if I have to, but I swear to God, I will find—"

"Okay, Rhys. Okay." West grabbed his pack mate's shoulders, cutting off his tirade. Rhys dragged in a rough breath, his body shaking with suppressed energy. "We'll go to

Salt Lake. We'll get closer. But we can't move on anything until we know for sure. We can't afford to be sloppy about this, brother."

"If we are, we'll only risk Sariah getting hurt," Noah put in softly. He'd risen from his chair too, his gray eyes swirling with worry. "Or killed."

Rhys grimaced, his face contorting with frustration and pain. My heart ached for him. He'd spent years, much longer than I'd even known him, being told the same thing over and over by his pack mates. And they weren't wrong. Getting Sariah back would be difficult, and their attack on the Austin complex had proven that any missteps or wrong guesses could be disastrous.

But how long could he have patience? How long could he keep the flame of hope alive under a constant barrage of setbacks?

I knew all too well what that felt like, and I wished I could fix this for him. Make things better somehow.

But I could barely even control my wolf. And although I'd been able to get him partway to finding his sister, I couldn't grant him the missing pieces.

"I know." Rhys clenched his jaw, his shoulders falling as his head drooped slightly. "I just want to be there. If something happens, and I wasn't there for her..."

He trailed off, looking ill. I stepped out of Jackson's embrace and wrapped my arms around Rhys's waist, resting my head on his chest.

I half expected him to push me away, to yell at me that this was my fault for delivering half-formed information. But instead, his thick arms came around me, squeezing me to him so tight I almost couldn't breathe as he buried his face in my hair.

He clung to me as if he needed me. As if I truly could help him—not by delivering up his sister, but just by being here for him.

Tears pricked the backs of my eyes, and I held onto his muscled form for dear life, offering up what little strength I had. West's hand fell on Rhys's shoulder, lending his comfort too.

"Jesus. You guys were telling the truth? Strand did this to you all?"

Carl's voice broke the silence, and I looked over to him, startled. I'd honestly forgotten he and Molly were even here. He was staring at the TV through narrowed eyes, chewing on his bottom lip.

"Yeah. We were telling the truth," Noah said tiredly.

"And that's who has your sister?" Carl shifted his gaze to Rhys.

I wasn't surprised Molly had told him everything I'd told her about our situation. Or maybe the guys had told him at some point. There really wasn't any reason to hide the truth anymore.

"Yeah." The single word seemed to cause Rhys physical pain.

I pulled away as he spoke, glancing up at his face. His expression was wary, but his voice was calmer, less wild.

The wiry, sharp-faced man hesitated for a second. Then

he glanced at Molly before nodding decisively. "Then I'll help you get her out."

"*What?*"

I probably shouldn't have blurted it out like that, and I definitely shouldn't have let so much disbelief color my tone. But just a few days ago, Carl had been unwilling to even let us back inside the house. Now he was offering to help us with a dangerous, maybe impossible, mission? Why?

Rhys shifted to face him, keeping an arm draped over my shoulder as he narrowed his eyes. "Yeah, what?"

Carl shook his head, his lips tilting up a little at our obvious disbelief. "Hey, man. I didn't just become a fuckin' saint or anything. But I know what it's like to have someone try to take what you love away from you." His hand found Molly's, and she leaned into him, burrowing against his shoulder. "It's not fucking right. And besides, we're not staying in Vegas. Not after the shit that went down today. We need a fresh start somewhere."

His voice was rough, and I realized he was serious. He would leave everything behind to keep her safe.

"I'm not gonna lie, we could really use your help, Carl." Noah spoke carefully, his brows pinched together. "But are you sure? We're going up against a massive corporation with resources to spare. We were lucky we managed to get Alexis out of the Austin complex where we found her—and Strand hasn't stopped hunting us since. You don't have to get involved. You and Molly have already done enough."

The wiry man chuckled. "Well, I'm not offering to go in with you, guns blazing. That's never really been my style. But it sounds like you need information and resources. *That,* I can definitely do."

Molly turned her head to lay a kiss on his shoulder. "I'll help too, if I can."

"Thank you," I whispered, gratitude and relief unwinding some of the tension in my chest.

Carl wrapped his arms around Molly, pulling her into his lap. The way he touched her reminded me of how my mates were with me—as if even a hair's-breadth of space between us was sometimes too much.

"You don't need to thank me. Like I said, I owe you." His expression hardened. "I'd have given anything to kill the cocksuckers who took Molly myself. But having their throats ripped out by a giant fucking wolf is the death they deserved."

His tone was fierce, almost proud, but his harsh words made my stomach twist.

I'd killed three men today, and when I was finished, my wolf had been hungry for more.

Was this really who I was becoming?

CHAPTER SEVENTEEN

None of us would've chosen to tell Carl and Molly about the Strand experiments and the existence of shifters, but it turned out to be the best thing that could've happened.

With Carl's help, information that had been impossible for the guys to dig up on their own suddenly became much more accessible—not to mention, the pawn shop owner had access to false identification, weapons, and other gear. I'd always known the pawn shop was basically a front for his other "businesses", but I hadn't really wrapped my head around what he truly did for a living.

As Molly explained to me in a quiet voice while Carl and my mates put their heads together to confer, her boyfriend was a sort of "fixer." What that meant depended on what whoever came to him needed—it could be anything from forging documents to hacking computers to money laundering.

My gaze flicked to him across the room, gesturing animatedly as he talked, and I cocked my head slightly. He looked almost exactly like the stereotypical mobsters I'd seen in dozens of movies and TV shows, but... not. Although he could be terrifying when he was angry, there was a softness that came into his eyes from time to time, especially when he looked at Molly. Whether he'd developed his softer side after falling in love with her or she fell in love with him *because* of that softer side, I wasn't sure. And really, it didn't matter.

I was just grateful whatever moral code Carl lived by had prompted him to offer us help.

The seven of us migrated to the kitchen eventually. We ordered pizza and began working out a plan while Carl tapped away on his laptop, green eyes darting quickly back and forth as he scanned the screen. The guys really hadn't been able to dig up much useful information on the Strand complex in Salt Lake, so once we had more to go on, there were a lot of details to work out.

Time seemed to slide by as if someone had greased the wheels, and when I finally glanced up at the clock, it was already after 11 p.m.

Rhys had argued successfully that we should leave the next day. Any last minute adjustments to our plan would be easier to make once we were closer to our target, and it was better if we left Vegas before anyone connected Molly and me to the three mauled bodies in a house on the far side of the city.

There was more to do. So much more. And I really

wanted to be a contributing member of the team, but as the evening wore on, my focus began to slip.

My wolf, still agitated from the events of the day, paced and whined inside me, like a dog who couldn't decide if she wanted to be inside or outside. She was restless, irritable, and unsettled. I found myself terrified that she would burst out again at any moment, tearing apart the delicate partnership we'd established with Molly and Carl.

I didn't think she would attack anyone here, but I still didn't feel like I could trust her completely, and I hated that.

Shifting uncomfortably in my seat, I rubbed at my chest as if the wolf inside me was a bad case of heartburn. Noah noticed and rested a hand on my knee, leaning in to speak low in my ear as the others continued talking around us.

"You should get some rest. We'll keep hammering out details, but we can get by without you for a bit. You went through a lot today. Give your wolf some time to calm down."

I looked up into his gray-blue eyes, wishing I was strong enough to tell him I didn't need a break. None of them were resting, and I was sure Nils and his team of hunters weren't either. This wasn't a game for weaklings.

But he was right. I could feel my control slipping, and it would be worse if I pushed through and let something terrible happen.

"Okay. Thanks. Come get me if you need anything though, all right?"

"We will." He pulled me toward him, pressing a soft kiss to my lips, then nudged me gently in the direction of the door.

Rhys looked up as I left, nodding in understanding. His eyes hadn't stopped blazing with a fevered excitement since Carl had agreed to help us, and even though he didn't judge me for resting, I was sure it would be hours before *he* went to sleep.

I padded down the hall to the guest bedroom and closed the door behind me before stripping off my shirt and jeans. I rummaged in the large closet we all shared, caving to my impulse and grabbing one of West's t-shirts. It hung down to my mid-thighs, and it smelled just like him—woodsy and clean. The scent comforted me. I felt so distant from him, and even though Jackson had helped me understand why his pack mate kept pulling away, it didn't stop the yearning in my soul.

Now that my body knew sleep was coming, a wave of exhaustion crashed over me, making my feet drag as I shuffled across the room and practically face-planted on the mattress.

But as soon as I nestled under the covers, doubts and fears crawled inside my mind like monsters that had been hiding under the bed. Despite the softness of the pillow and the comforting weight of the heavy blanket, my eyes refused to stay closed.

Quiet sounds filtered into the room from down the hall, and I tried to let the comforting baritone of my mates' voices soothe me.

I wasn't sure how long I lay like that, trying to find sleep, but when the door creaked as it opened a while later, I was still wide awake. Noah poked his head through the crack, and when he caught my gaze, he stepped inside, closing the door softly behind him.

"Can't sleep?"

I shook my head, relieved to be dragged out of my own whirling thoughts. "No."

He crossed to the bed and sat beside me, reaching out to run his fingers along my cheek. My eyelids drooped at his touch, and I turned my head slightly to chase the feeling. It was almost like a drug, one I would happily get high on over and over again.

"What's on your mind, Scrubs? Can I help?"

His voice was full of concern and caring, and I wanted to drown in everything that was Noah. From the first day I'd met him—when I still thought his name was Cliff—he'd been taking care of me, and I knew he always would. I reached up and tugged on his hand, urging him to lie down next to me. He did, stretching out his large body beside mine. The blankets still separated us, but I could feel the delicious strength and heat of his muscles as he draped an arm over me, enclosing me in his embrace.

"My wolf is acting strange. She's upset, restless, and I don't know what to do about it," I admitted, turning my head to meet his gaze. "When I attacked those men, when I killed them... I was worried I wouldn't be able to stop."

He rested his head on the pillow next to mine, our faces only inches apart. "But you did. You didn't hurt Molly."

The mere thought of it sent shivers racing up my spine, and I grimaced. "Thank God."

"You went through a lot today, Scrubs. I wish we could've been there for you. I know you can take care of yourself, but I wish I could've killed those men so you didn't have to."

I inhaled his scent as our combined breath filled the space between us. Just his presence was calming me down, soothing my wolf. I sighed, feeling the tension in my shoulders start to unwind. "I feel so out of control most of the time. My wolf is so big, so powerful. I could be a huge help to you guys, but I worry I'll always just be a mess you have to keep cleaning up."

"Nah. Jackson's already claimed that position."

Noah laughed softly, and I chuckled. Jackson was notorious for pulling crazy stunts when he needed to blow off steam, something his pack mates had learned to deal with before he did anything truly insane.

"Yeah, I'll probably never top him. I just feel like..." I rubbed my chest again, the ache there growing in intensity as I spoke about it. "Like I need something. Like something is missing, somehow."

Noah rose up on one elbow, leaning over me with a look of concern. "What, Scrubs? What do you need?"

You.

It was the truest, simplest answer to his question. The mate bond between me and the four shifter men pulled at me every day, reminding me that although they were mine and I was theirs, our connection wasn't yet complete.

I needed him. In a basic, primal way that went so far beyond sex it reached a soul level.

Noah was my mate, my first crush, my savior. He was one of four people in the entire world that I trusted without a shadow of a doubt—that I would lay down my life to protect, if it came to it. His boyish face and sculpted muscles were almost inhumanly beautiful, but it was what was *inside* that made me want to wrap myself in his embrace and never come up for air.

I couldn't find the words to express my scattered thoughts or the aching need that bloomed in my chest every time I was around my men. So I answered without words, lifting my head off the pillow and pressing a kiss to his full, soft lips.

Noah responded immediately. He cradled the back of my head with a large hand, bringing me closer as he returned the kiss. His tongue brushed against mine, making sparks fly through my body and throbbing heat gather in my core. His body moved over mine as he kissed me, pinning me to the bed under the blanket that still separated us. I fought against the stupid thing, wanting to wrap my legs around him, to hold onto him forever.

Gently, he lowered my head back down to the pillow, trailing his fingers down my neck, over my collarbone, along the curve of my breast as he devoured me with his kiss.

"Noah!" I gasped, finally working my arms out from under the blanket to twine them around his shoulders.

"Oh God, Alexis."

He moved against me, and I could feel the hard bulge of his cock pressing against my core, promising something so sweet and overwhelming I was afraid it might destroy me.

But I would happily risk annihilation.

I moved against him, urging him on as our tongues danced with each other, tasting and savoring.

Then, with a grunt, Noah tore himself away from my lips, sucking in a deep breath as he drew back. Even in the shadowy light, I could see the battle raging in his soft gray eyes. He was trying to master himself. To pull away like they always did.

Panic flooded my chest as I gazed up at him, already feeling the cold emptiness of the dark room, the sting of his rejection.

But I wasn't injured anymore. I was healthy. I was fine.

And I was desperate.

"No! Noah, please! Don't go. Please!" I hauled his face back down to mine, peppering his skin with kisses while I spoke. "I need you. I need you so fucking much. Please don't leave me. Don't go."

His body tensed for a moment, and then he pulled back slightly again, staring at the tears that leaked from my eyes. I blinked them away, my breath coming in soft gasps as I locked eyes with him.

Slowly, deliberately, Noah pulled my hands away from his shoulders, pressing them down into the pillow above my head.

My heart fell as he leaned away from me, scooting toward the edge of the bed. He stepped off it, and I tried to bolster myself against the heartache, unfulfilled need, and loneliness that I knew would smother me as soon as he left.

But he didn't leave.

Instead, he reached down and grabbed the comforter in a tight fist before tearing it off the bed.

CHAPTER EIGHTEEN

The cool air of the bedroom met my skin in a rush, making goose bumps skitter over my body. The oversized t-shirt I'd worn to bed had worked its way up, and now the hem was bunched around my waist, leaving my soft blue panties exposed.

Noah still held the edge of the comforter in one fist. His gaze swept over my body, the expression on his face so heated that it banished any memory of the cold. I bit my lip, watching him watch me, as wetness dampened my panties. I shifted, bringing my legs together a little, squeezing my knees to try to relieve the building ache.

The beautiful man before me let out a noise that was almost a growl, dropping the blanket as he crawled back onto the bed. He pulled my legs apart, settling himself between them, and despite the fierce hunger in his eyes, his touch was gentle.

"No, Scrubs. Let me. I'll take care of you."

I wasn't even quite sure what that meant, but the promise in his voice made shivers of desire run through my body. And I trusted him, more than I'd ever trusted anyone in my life. Pushing my nerves aside, I let the muscles in my legs relax, allowing him to move them however he liked.

He grinned at me as he felt the change in my body, and rewarded my compliance by pressing a kiss to the inside of my knee. I'd never been particularly conscious of that part of my anatomy before, but the touch of his lips and the soft scrape of his stubble against the sensitive skin there exploded through every single nerve ending I had.

I gasped, arching off the bed. Noah grinned wider and did it again, trailing his mouth slowly upward over my heated flesh, alternating between legs so I never knew where the touch would come next. By the time his warm breath ghosted over my panties, I was a writhing, panting mess.

The fabric was soaked. I could feel it, and a momentary flash of embarrassment flooded me. Was I supposed to be this wet?

But any shame or awkwardness I felt slipped away when Noah kissed me through the fabric of my panties, then clamped his mouth down and sucked. Pleasure slammed into me like a runaway train, and my upper body came all the way off the bed as I clutched at his head, trying to—I wasn't even sure what. Bring him closer? Push him away so I could breathe again?

Noah lifted his head, licking his lips as he smiled up at me. He slid a hand up my body and under the oversized shirt to the space right between my breasts, then pressed slowly on my sternum to make me lie back down. He kept his hand right there, using his other to work my panties over my hips and down my legs. I bent my knees to help him, my chest rising and falling fast under his palm as nerves and excitement raged through my veins.

When he'd bared my lower half, Noah dipped his head between my legs again. This time, when his mouth met my core, there was nothing between us. His warm, wet tongue licked a path up my slick folds to my clit as the hand on my chest slid over to my breast, rolling and pinching my nipple.

"Oh God!" I bit my lip, squeezing my eyes shut against the torrent of sensations, vaguely aware that my cry had been way too loud not to be heard down the hall.

But Noah didn't stop. He ran the flat of his tongue over my clit before swirling it over the small bud in a pattern that left me breathless. One hand continued to tease and play with my nipple while the other held onto my hip, holding me still while he lapped at me.

He released his grip on my side, and a moment later, a long, thick finger slid inside me. My core clamped around the invasion instinctively, needing more of that pressure, that exquisite fullness.

The feelings inside me were building to a peak, pushing to the top of a precipice as he fucked me with his finger and worshipped me with his mouth. I was so close to coming.

Then... he stopped.

He pulled away from me, slowly sliding his finger out. My eyes flew open, and I stared down my body at him in shock.

His lips quirked in the lopsided smile I loved so much as he pressed little kisses to my clit and the insides of my thighs, making me quiver with unspent tension.

"I don't want you to come yet. For your first time, it might make you too tight, and I don't want to hurt you."

I nodded, barely understanding his words through my haze of lust. I wasn't surprised he knew I was a virgin. I couldn't even be mad that Rhys or West had told him—it was probably why my mates had been so reluctant to touch me while I was recovering from my injuries. None of them had wanted to hurt me.

But this didn't hurt.

It felt so fucking good.

And thank God, one of us knew what they were doing, because I certainly didn't. I was grateful Noah was taking the lead, guiding me through this. Grateful my first time would be with someone who had experience.

That thought caused an unexpected twinge of pain in my chest, and I blinked back the sudden sting of tears.

"What?" Noah noticed the shift in my expression immediately, and his brows drew together, concern darkening his features. "What is it, Scrubs? Are you okay?"

I nodded quickly, forcing a smile to my face to assure him he hadn't done anything wrong. Everything he'd done was perfect. "Yeah. More than okay. I was just thinking I was glad you'll be my first. And then I thought..." I swallowed, forcing the words out. "I wish... I could've been *your* first."

A heartbreakingly tender expression crossed his face, and he crawled up my body to hover over me, gazing down into my eyes. "Fuck. Me too, Scrubs. So much. I won't lie and say I've never had sex before, but... if I knew you were out there, I would've waited. I would've waited for you my whole damn life."

Noah's words landed right in my heart, expanding it until it felt too big for the confined cavity of my chest.

God, I loved this man.

His sweetness. His strength. His sincerity.

With an inarticulate sound, I reached for him, wrapping my arms around his shoulders and kissing him like I'd never get enough. He was still dressed, but I could feel the heat of his skin even through the layers of fabric that separated us.

He sank into the kiss, settling his body onto mine but being sure not to crush me. The fire that had been building inside me earlier began to flare again, and I wrapped my legs around him, pressing my heels against his firm ass to pin his body to mine. His cock ground against my core, and I knew I was probably leaving a wet stain on the front of his pants, but I didn't give a single shit about that right now.

Noah tore his mouth away from mine, gasping for air. "Oh fuck, Scrubs. I'm trying to take this slow, but you're making it hard as hell."

A chuckle burst from my lips, and I squeezed his lean waist between my thighs. "Literally?"

His smile was teasing but heavy with desire as he moved against me slightly, showing me exactly what I was doing to him. "Yes, literally."

He drew back slightly, but before I could protest the space between us, he reached for the hem of my shirt. I arched my back and raised my hands, allowing him to pull it over my head. The t-shirt ended up somewhere on the floor as Noah tossed it away carelessly, his gaze riveted to me.

I settled back against the sheets, my hands still draped over my head, my entire body bared to him.

He'd seen me naked before. I knew he had.

When they'd found me after the ambulance crash, I hadn't had a stitch of clothing on. But this was different, and the look in his eyes made me certain he felt it too.

His gaze trailed over me as if he were trying to soak up every single detail of my form. For a moment, I let myself bask in his attention, my clit throbbing and my nipples aching from the pure want in his blue eyes.

"This really isn't fair, you know," I murmured, sitting up on my elbows and watching his gaze darken with desire as he tracked the movement. "I'm totally naked, and you're wearing way too many clothes."

With a seductive smile, he pulled his shirt off with one hand, baring the sculpted muscles of his arms, shoulders, and abs. The room was dark, but moonlight spilled through the curtains, highlighting the contours of his body in shades of gray and blue.

He was fucking beautiful.

When he moved to unbutton his jeans, I scrambled to my knees to help. He dropped his hands to his sides, the muscles of his abs bunching and contracting as he allowed me to take over.

I popped the button and tugged the zipper down

carefully, then drew his briefs and jeans down together, freeing his cock.

It was thick, slightly curved, and smooth as silk in my hand. He groaned when I closed my fingers around the shaft, and the vein that ran along the top pulsed slightly.

I had no real idea what I was doing, but I liked the feel of his hard length in my hand, liked getting a chance to explore him. His cock was strange but sort of beautiful, with small drops of liquid leaking from the slit at the tip.

And most of all, I liked how he reacted to my touch.

It fed the ravenous hunger inside me, and the muscles of my core clenched, making my clit throb harder.

Tentatively, I reached out and swiped my tongue over the broad head, lapping up the liquid that had gathered there. It was salty and tangy, and when I closed my mouth around the whole thing, Noah let out a choked growl.

"Fuck, Alexis. Fuck."

He sounded almost pained. Like it was sweet torture for him to have my lips wrapped around him. I bobbed my head a few times, using my saliva to smooth out the movement. It felt clumsy and awkward, but I felt his hips twitch beneath my hands, and more of those sounds I was learning to love fell from his mouth.

"Jesus. I'm gonna come if you keep that up." He pushed gently on my shoulders, making me stop. "And this is about you, beautiful. I want to make this good for you."

"It is. I like this," I panted breathlessly, my hips shifting of their own accord, seeking something to quell the demanding ache inside me.

He'd worked me right up to the edge with his tongue, and my body was trapped on that peak like a rollercoaster at the top of an incline, desperate for release. I was tempted to reach between my legs and take care of things myself, but I knew there was something much better, much sweeter, waiting for me.

"Goddamn, Scrubs. You're so fucking perfect."

He cupped the sides of my face, pulling me up so we were kneeling together on the bed before claiming my mouth in another fierce kiss. I could taste myself on his tongue, and I wondered if he could taste his essence on mine. A whimper escaped my throat at the thought.

Jesus, that's hot.

Without breaking the contact of our lips, Noah lowered me back down to the mattress, positioning himself over me. He reached down with one hand and guided his cock to my entrance, using the thick head to tease my clit again. A spasm of almost blinding pleasure spiked through my body, and my mouth fell open.

"I can't wait any longer, Scrubs," he murmured, his lips brushing my jaw. "I need to be inside you. I'll go slow, okay?"

Slow. Fast. I didn't care, as long as he gave me what I needed. I nodded desperately, my hands skating across his back, my legs hooking around his waist again.

And then his cock was at my entrance, pushing slowly inside.

It was big. Much bigger than his finger.

He pressed in inch by agonizing inch, until I felt him hit the barrier inside me. He pulled back slowly, his face hovering inches from mine as he gazed into my eyes. Then he dipped his head to kiss me again as his hips surged forward.

There was a sharp twinge of pain, and my muscles contracted involuntarily, a gasp tearing from my lips. He stilled, giving me time to adjust to the size of him.

"All right?" he whispered.

I nodded, my heart slamming hard against my ribs at the enormity of this moment. Of what it meant for me. For him.

For us.

Noah was fully seated inside me, his cock stretching my inner walls, his pelvic bone pressed against mine. That pressure sent sparks ricocheting through my body, and I bumped my hips against his, seeking more friction.

He responded to my urging, drawing back slowly only to slide in again, increasing the sensations cascading through me. He set up a steady rhythm, bracing himself on his forearms as he thrust into me over and over.

There was a slight, lingering pain from his first penetration, but that only seemed to heighten the pleasure flooding my body. Noah's face was taut, and a sheen of sweat dampened his forehead as he fucked me.

When he moved one hand down between us and found my clit again, it was too much. The tension that had been building inside me snapped like a whip as I came hard.

"Noah! Oh—fuck!"

I threw my head back, my body arching off the bed as my inner muscles clamped down around his cock in rhythmic waves.

"Goddamn, Alexis. God... I'm coming."

He thrust into me hard two more times then stilled, his body shaking as he emptied himself inside me.

I could feel wetness leaking out from the place where we were connected as he collapsed on top of me. He didn't brace himself this time, and the heavy weight of his body pressed me into the mattress. But it was the best thing I'd ever felt.

Finally, he lifted his head, smoothing my sweat-dampened hair away from my face and kissing me again with slow, lazy strokes of his tongue. Then he drew back, gazing down at me intently. "You still okay?"

A soft chuckle fell from my lips. "Are you kidding? I think you ruined me."

His eyes widened, and he reared back farther. "What? Are you all right? I—"

I wrapped my arms around him, pulling him down on top of my body again. He was still inside me, his cock slowly softening, but I wasn't ready to let this connection go yet.

"In the best way, Noah. That was... incredible."

The tension drained from his body, and he rolled over onto his back, pulling me on top of him. "Jesus, Scrubs. Don't scare me like that. Do you have any idea how fucking nervous I was?"

"*You* were nervous?" I scrunched up my face. "Why would you be nervous? I was the one who had no idea what she was doing."

"Trust me, you improvised just fine." He smirked playfully, sliding a hand down my back to cup my ass. Then his expression grew serious. "I just didn't want to mess it up, you know? You're special. You deserved something special for your first time."

"It was." I rested my head on his chest, listening to the quiet thud of his heart. "It was perfect."

He held me like that as our heartbeats slowed together, our bodies moving in sync as we breathed. All the doubts, fears, and worries that had haunted my mind earlier went silent, washed away by blissful exhaustion. Right now, it was just me and Noah, connected in the most primal way, bound up in each other body and soul.

I was vaguely aware that at some point, he pulled out of me, settling me gently onto the mattress beside him. He slid to the end of the bed to retrieve the comforter and drew it over us, then wrapped his arms around me and pulled me into the cradle of his body.

My wolf whuffed contentedly, and a sleepy smile crossed my lips. For the first time in days, she felt peaceful, calm, and as sated as I was.

Hell, she *was* as sated as I was.

Because whether I was ready to admit it or not, she was a part of me.

CHAPTER NINETEEN

When the alarm clock blared, I jerked awake and groaned, peeling my scratchy eyes open.

"Aw, fuck."

Jackson's voice was rough with sleep, and a second later, a shoe sailed across the room, missing the offending alarm on the nightstand by about a foot. It fell to the floor as I leaned over, straining against Noah's grip on me to hit the snooze button. The blinking red panel read 6:01.

Noah yawned, pulling me back into the warmth of his embrace as quiet fell over the room again. I felt his cock pressing against my ass as he spooned me, and memories of last night flooded my mind.

I could still feel him everywhere, as if he'd marked me permanently somehow. There was a slight ache between my legs, and my muscles were a little sore—similar to how they would've felt the day after a hard workout with Erin back at the Strand complex.

Except Erin's workouts were never this fun.

As if he'd been reliving last night right along with me, Noah lifted his head, nipping at my earlobe before murmuring, "Morning, beautiful."

I let out a happy, contented little noise, moving my hips against him encouragingly.

"No fucking time for morning sex," Rhys growled from the other side of the room, and I yelped.

Despite having just heard Jackson speak, I'd sort of forgotten that the other guys were all here, arrayed around the floor in makeshift blanket nests. They'd let me and Noah have the bed, and we were both still naked under the covers.

Waking up in one man's arms surrounded by three other men should've felt incredibly awkward, but somehow, it wasn't.

They were all my mates. I felt the same pull toward each of them that I felt toward Noah, and we all knew it.

"Come on! We gotta get moving." Rhys was already up and dressed, stuffing clothes hurriedly into one of our packs.

Noah leaned up onto his elbow, rolling me onto my back and looking down at me with a smile brighter than sunshine. Ignoring the manic energy that poured off Rhys, he leaned down to kiss me softly. His gray-blue eyes shone as he whispered, in a voice so low it was meant only for me, "That was the best night of my life, Scrubs. Hands down. I'll never forget it."

I bit my lip, nodding in agreement. There was so much more I wanted to say—to him and to all the men in this room —but now wasn't the time. Rhys had finished with one pack and was striding around the room, grabbing up more items to stuff into the second.

With a sigh, Noah threw the covers back and slid out of bed, snagging a fresh set of clothes before Rhys could pack those too. I followed, still nowhere near as comfortable with casual nudity as these guys were. My hands itched to cover my boobs as I padded softly across the room, but I forced myself to act natural and let my arms hang loosely by my sides.

It didn't help that the entire room seemed to hold its breath as soon as I stepped out of bed. I swore I could feel the temperature of the air rising as Jackson's gaze locked on me. West dropped his chin, but I could see his dark eyes watching me through his thick lashes. Rhys paused in his mad packing dash, tugging his lower lip between his teeth.

Even Noah, who'd seen me naked plenty last night, stared at me with heat in his eyes as if it were the first time.

My skin prickled, flushing with desire as my body responded to their looks. Warmth pooled in my low belly, and my core clenched.

Trying to pretend everything was perfectly normal and that I wasn't ridiculously turned on, I grabbed for some clothes blindly, turning around to look at the guys only once I had a bra and panties on. Judging by their expressions, my outfit change hadn't helped diffuse the situation very much.

Blushing furiously, I tugged on my jeans and cleared my throat. "Sorry I skipped out early last night. Do we have a plan?"

"Um..." Rhys seemed to have temporarily lost the power

of speech. Finally, he shook himself, tearing his gaze away from me and looking down at the large backpack in his hands as if he had no idea how it'd gotten there. "We're heading out soon. Carl called in a favor to get us a clean vehicle in a hurry, and he's got a hacker friend of his digging up more info on Strand. We've got more info on the complex itself, and we'll work out the details on the way to Salt Lake City."

"Sounds good."

I joined him in packing as the others gathered their things. We'd picked up extra clothes since arriving in Vegas, and West shoved them into a suitcase he must've gotten from Molly.

When the alarm went off again at 6:10, we were all ready. Jackson smacked the button on top with satisfaction, his eyes still squinty with sleep.

"Too fucking early," he muttered.

"You can sleep on the way," West told him, hefting one of the bags over his shoulders.

We joined Molly in the kitchen. Empty pizza boxes and a few beer bottles sat on the counter, remnants of last night's planning session, and someone had picked up a to-go order of donuts and coffee.

"Carl here?" Jackson asked, perking up a little as he grabbed a donut in each hand.

"He's getting the car." Molly smoothed her hands down the front of her pants before tucking a stray lock of honey-blonde hair behind her ear.

She seemed anxious and pensive, and it struck me what a

huge thing this was for her. She was about to leave her entire life behind—just walk away from all of it and close the door on her way out, as if she'd never been here at all.

She didn't have family to speak of. She'd told me both her parents had died several years ago of different types of cancer. But still. She was about to untether herself completely from the life she knew and throw herself into the unknown.

She'd never see the hospital where she worked again.

Never see her friends or coworkers.

Never see this house.

I could relate to that kind of upheaval and what it did to one's mental and emotional state.

Bypassing the coffee and donuts, I stepped over to Molly and reached for her tentatively. I didn't want to scare her—she'd seen me maul three grown men yesterday, after all—but when she didn't flinch away, I pulled her into a tight hug.

She let out a shuddering breath, wrapping her arms around me too.

"I'm sorry, Molly," I said softly. "About everything."

"It's for the best." Her voice was steady, but tinged with sadness. When we broke apart, determination flashed in her blue-green eyes. "If we don't leave, Carl won't be able to let this go. He'll go after Travis's friends, and their friends. He'll get himself locked in a war he'll never get out of. I can't let that happen. I can't lose him."

I nodded, a lump rising in my throat. The way Carl and Molly loved each other made my heart ache. She would do anything for him, and he'd do the same for her, even if it meant abandoning their old lives to start over together somewhere. It didn't matter; their true home was each other.

We broke apart, each pulling ourselves back together before we dissolved into weepy messes. This wasn't the time for that.

"Here, Alexis. Fuel for the road."

Jackson had polished off his pair of donuts and now held two out to me, grinning widely. He always teased me about how much I could pack away in my small frame, but at the moment, I was just grateful he knew me well enough to know I'd definitely want two donuts... to start.

I accepted them gratefully, finishing the first off in three bites as Jackson chuckled. I ate the second a little slower, and by the time I'd finished my third and grabbed a cup of coffee, the front door banged shut in the living room.

A moment later, Carl poked his head into the kitchen. "Got the car. You all ready?"

There was a chorus of agreement, and Jackson and I both made another mad dash for the donuts before we followed Carl outside. He'd picked up a large blue van, which was more than enough to accommodate the seven of us, considering we were all traveling extremely light. I had no idea if he and Molly were really planning to abandon all their stuff, or if he'd had have one of his many underground contacts pack it up and deliver it to them wherever they ended up. But at the moment, all they had was a single bag each.

Rhys insisted on driving. His face was set into a tight mask, and I could feel the tension pouring from him. It reminded me of how he'd acted when I first met him, although now, despite his intensity, none of his anger was directed toward me.

As we pulled onto Interstate 15 out of the city, I glanced at Carl, who'd taken the front passenger seat. "Were you able to dig up much more info about Strand?"

He ran a hand over his slicked-back hair. "Some, yeah. From the looks of things, they've kept a tight lid on their operation. They must've, to have been able to conduct human experiments like this for so many years without word of it getting out. I had a hacker friend of mine do some digging, but even he didn't find much. They've got the money and the resources to have the latest tech for everything, but it looks like they did a lot of stuff the old fashioned way—paper and ink, in person meetings, stuff like that."

"What difference does that make?"

"Makes information easier to control. Once something's digital, it's harder to keep it from leaking. But if you've got watermarked paper documents? And only a few copies of those? You can keep things a lot closer to the vest."

"Oh."

I sank back into my seat, leaning against Noah's shoulder. A sudden vivid image of a blood-splattered piece of paper bearing Sariah's name popped into my head, and I winced at the memory. I'd been so delirious at the time, it hadn't even occurred to me to question why a company like Strand, which could afford to build an entire self-sustaining underground medical complex to house just a few test subjects, would use something as basic as a simple spreadsheet to track their experiments.

"So, are we out of luck then?"

Carl half-turned in his seat, his sharp features splitting into a grin. "Far from it, sweetheart. Whether you go old-school or new-school for information storage, you can't ever get rid of the human element. And that's where the cracks show up in even the most airtight operations. Granted, there weren't a lot of cracks to find in this case—Strand either pays their people obscenely well, blackmails them, or both. Or, fuck, they could do some kind of memory wipe on anyone they think is a risk. If they can turn people into damn wolves, who knows what else they can do."

His gaze flicked from me to Noah, and he shook his head as if he couldn't quite believe what he'd just said. Then he continued.

"Like I said, there wasn't much out there. But"—he beamed proudly—"my buddy managed to dig up blueprints to a facility in Salt Lake that sounds a lot like the one the guys say you were in. Hundred bucks it's the Strand complex. I've got my contact digging for more info now, but it's a start."

I blinked, conflicting emotions welling inside me. On the one hand, that was amazing news. The guys had tried to find information for months and had gotten nowhere, so this was a huge win.

But on the other hand, the idea of stepping foot inside a facility like the one I'd grown up in made me want to vomit. I still had nightmares most nights about that place, the once comforting walls harsh and foreboding in my subconscious mind.

Could I handle it? Would I be able to put aside my own traumatic memories to focus on Sariah's rescue? Or would my panic allow my wolf to take over entirely, risking our whole operation?

Stop it, Alexis! Don't even think like that.

Something had shifted inside me last night after Noah and I had sex. I wasn't sure if it was just because my wolf had finally gotten what she wanted—or part of it, anyway—but she seemed calmer now. And she felt different, more like a true part of me and less like some strange alien entity merely existing inside me.

I had to have faith that if I kept trying, I'd be able to make peace with my wolf, to become one with her so that when I shifted, my human side wasn't shoved down like a rock sinking to the bottom of a lake. So that *I* remained in control, even in wolf form.

"Anyway, we'll be able to analyze the blueprints for entrances and exits, layout, and structural weaknesses," Carl went on, dragging my attention back to the present.

He was in his element now, eyes blazing with excitement as he talked about his plans for getting us inside the complex, and how we could use Strand's old-school security technology to our advantage. My brows drew together as I listened intently, trying to make sense of everything he was saying.

I wasn't sure when it had happened, but somewhere

along the line, our fight against Strand had become his fight too.

Now we just had to pray his help would get us through this alive.

CHAPTER TWENTY

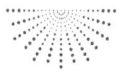

The drive to Salt Lake City was only about six hours long, but we stopped midway, exiting onto a small side road in what felt like the middle of nowhere.

I'd been dozing, propped up between Noah and Jackson, but the change in our speed roused me. I blinked out the window, stifling a yawn. I hadn't gotten much sleep last night —none of us had, really—but I couldn't regret that. Nothing could've been more worth it.

"What's going on? Why are we stopping?"

"You need practice," West said firmly from the back seat.

I craned my neck to look at him, surprised when he actually met my eyes. "What?"

"West doesn't want you to break into Strand with us when we get to Salt Lake. He doesn't think it's safe." Jackson wrinkled his nose.

"*What?*"

"I'm just trying to keep her, and us, from getting hurt,"

West said stoically. "I don't know why you're all so willing to let her risk herself like this."

"I want to!" I blurted quickly. I'd be damned if I was going to sit this fight out, and I had to make sure all the guys knew I didn't need protecting when it came to this rescue mission. "I want to help!"

"We know, Scrubs." Noah's voice was gentle, although worry lurked in the depths of his eyes. "And none of us are going to tell you what you can and can't do. But we just want to make sure you're as ready as possible."

"Yeah... Okay."

I shot another look toward the back seat. West's stubborn expression made me seriously doubt Noah's assurance that none of them would try to stop me from going with them.

We pulled to a stop near a lightly wooded area. No other cars were visible on the road, and I couldn't see any signs of civilization nearby. Jackson hopped out of the van, offering a hand to help me out too.

The others piled out behind us, although Molly and Carl hung back by the van while my men and I tromped deeper into the woods. I saw the two of them bending their heads over several sheets of printed paper and guessed they were going over the blueprints of the Strand complex. Then they disappeared from view, cut off by the trees as we walked farther away from the road.

"So, what now?" I asked when West and Rhys finally came to a stop.

"Now you shift." West crossed his arms over his chest.

I blanched. "What, right now? Just shift?"

Not bothering to respond with words, he peeled off his shirt, dropped his pants, and kicked off his shoes. I barely had time to absorb the sculpted lines of muscle under his mocha skin before he transformed. A few moments later, a wolf with gray markings and dark eyes gazed up at me, his expression somehow challenging.

So, yeah. Just shift.

Damn it. He made it look so easy.

But I understood the point he was trying to make. If I couldn't even control my wolf now, in a safe, no-pressure environment, how was I possibly supposed to keep her in line when my stress and adrenaline shot through the roof?

So I mimicked West's actions and stripped off my clothes, ignoring the tension that seemed to gather in the air as the cool breeze made my nipples pucker. I felt all the men's gazes on me, but I just closed my eyes, reaching inside me for the wild animal that lived there.

Deciding not to try force or coercion, I focused on what Noah had said about making peace with this part of myself. She still felt so alien, so *other*, sometimes. But maybe that wasn't true; maybe we weren't so different after all. With that thought in mind, I let myself become aware of what she was feeling and tried to allow myself to feel the same thing.

My head tilted to one side as I concentrated, letting my wolf inside my mind.

She wasn't uncomfortable with the men's attention at all. She reveled in it.

She knew, without any of the doubts or fears that plagued my human mind, that these men were hers.

She liked the feel of the earth beneath her feet, the tantalizing scents that drifted by on the breeze.

She was free.

Strong.

Unashamed and unapologetic.

I could be those things too, if only I'd allow myself to be.

With a snap, my bones cracked, changing and reforming under my skin as the shift finally took place. But this time, the pain wasn't as intense; it didn't feel like I was being torn apart. And within a few heartbeats, I blinked my eyes open to see that the colors of the world had shifted slightly like they always did when I was in wolf form.

I'd done it. I had shifted on command!

No. Not on command. *At will*. I hadn't had to command my wolf to do anything, and that was the whole point.

I yipped, a happy, excited sound. The dark gray wolf in front of me padded lightly forward, sniffing at me and licking at my fur. I felt the love and protectiveness in him as he nuzzled me—something I could barely detect in his human form these days.

A half-second later, the other three men around us began tearing off their clothes too, grins stretching across their faces. Even Rhys's mask of worry cracked for a moment as he joined in the celebration. As soon as they were naked, they each shifted—Jackson and Noah into pure white wolves, and Rhys into one with light gray markings.

Jackson threw back his head and howled, and Rhys nipped at him lightly. Probably warning him not to make too much noise. We were in a remote area, but there was no need to risk drawing attention to ourselves. Nils and his men were almost certainly still hunting us, and if anyone nearby happened to hear us and reported wolves in the area, I was sure he'd follow up on that lead like a bloodhound.

My mates all gathered around me, sniffing and whuffing. I couldn't see all of my own body, but I could tell I was almost a foot taller than them. The realization struck me as slightly hilarious, considering how much they towered over me in human form. It was like we'd reversed places somehow.

My tail wagged, and I leaned back on my haunches, stretching out my front legs. It felt good to be a wolf like this, surrounded by my mates. The scents of the forest called to me, and I lifted my nose into the air, sampling them all. When Jackson darted off among the trees, I followed him, loping easily on four legs. The others followed, flanking me on all sides as we raced through the woods.

The urge to howl rose up in my chest, so strong I almost couldn't hold it in. But I clamped my muzzle shut and settled for rolling onto my back when Jackson finally stopped in a clearing. Small twigs and rocks pressed into my fur, but my pelt was so thick I could hardly feel them.

A lupine face appeared above mine, Jackson's amber eyes shining down at me. He cocked his head, his tongue lolling out. Then... he pounced. We rolled over together, playfully snapping and batting at each other with our paws.

I was bigger and stronger than him in this form, but I was careful not to hurt him. It didn't take any effort at all—my wolf would never let that happen. I finally felt like I could trust that, at least.

What felt like way too soon, West let out a soft whine, calling our attention. We stood, shaking out our fur, and reluctantly followed him back to where we'd left our clothes. Noah and Jackson shifted back to human, looking lighter and happier as they dressed quickly. They'd needed this. We all had.

Nerves fluttered in my stomach as I stood by the small pile of clothes I'd left resting on my shoes. What if I couldn't shift back? It'd been difficult every other time I'd tried it. My wolf never seemed willing to cede control.

Rhys and West came to stand near me, lending me their support like their pack mates had the day I'd almost attacked Molly.

But I didn't want to have to rely on them for this. This was about my relationship with my wolf; I had to be able to do it on my own.

It's all right. You can stay, I whispered to her inside my soul. *Stay with me.*

Every other time I'd tried to shift back to human, I'd felt like I was trying to crawl out of my own skin, to escape the confines of the wolf form my human consciousness was lost in. But the truth was, there was nowhere to go. Everything I was—wolf, human, fighter, lover—was contained inside this single vessel.

There was no getting rid of my wolf.

She was me.

And I was her.

Stay. Stay.

The shift happened almost unconsciously, brief pain

rippling through my body before I found myself crouched on the forest floor, the chilly wind once again brushing my naked skin.

Before I could reach for my clothes, Jackson picked me up in a massive bear hug, spinning me around in a circle.

"That's my fucking girl! That was beautiful!"

He pressed his lips to mine, setting me back on my feet gently and bending me backward with the intensity of the kiss. When he pulled away, he was beaming and I was panting.

"Thanks, Jackson," I mumbled through tingling lips.

I stumbled over to my clothes on slightly wobbly legs, slipping everything back on before turning to look at West. He'd shifted back and dressed too, and the fabric of his dark t-shirt strained against his large biceps as he crossed his arms over his chest.

He looked torn between pride and disappointment as he regarded me, and I was sure I knew why. If I'd failed this test, he might've been able to talk the others into not letting me go with them on their rescue mission.

But I hadn't failed. I'd done it.

He pulled his bottom lip between his teeth, staring at me intently. Then a grin suddenly spread across his face like the sun breaking through a cloud as the twin dimples I loved so much appeared in his cheeks. It was the first time he'd smiled at me like that in weeks, and it was so potent it nearly knocked me on my ass.

"Well done, Scrubs. Well fucking done."

The rest of the journey was uneventful, though all the steam we'd blown off in the woods seemed to gather over us again like an angry raincloud as we drove in silence. Even Jackson was too tense to keep up his usual teasing litany of, "Are we there yet?"

I pored over the printouts of the Strand complex blueprints, trying to translate the strange lines and markings on the paper into physical walls and rooms in my mind's eye. From what I could gather, it was similar to the complex I'd lived in, at least in its basic shape. The complex was set up in several layers that went farther and farther underground, with each level spreading out in spokes from a central hub. There were small areas that might be offices or exam rooms, and several large, open spaces whose purpose was unclear.

Judging from the notes and markings on the blueprint, it was likely whoever had designed the building hadn't had any idea what the underground structure was going to be used for. Just another way Strand protected their secrets.

Carl spent most of the drive tapping away at his phone, lips pursed in concentration, while the rest of us discussed plans for how we'd get into the complex undetected—once we found out exactly *where* it was, anyway. The blueprints, as helpful as they were, gave us no clue where the complex was located.

That was the one missing piece in our plan, and with every mile that rolled away under us, the nervous churning of my stomach increased.

What would happen if we arrived in Salt Lake with no real clue where our target was? Rhys had threatened in anger to bang down every door in the city until he found what he was looking for, but that clearly wouldn't work in actual practice. And the longer we spent in the city, poking our noses where they didn't belong, the more likely it was that the Strand hunters would catch a whiff of what we were up to.

I had to suppress the urge to keep darting glances out the back window to make sure we weren't being followed. Where were Nils and his team now? Cleanup from the ambulance crash may have slowed them down, and they couldn't follow the tracking chip that'd been implanted under my skin anymore. But I was positive they were still searching for us. It was a miracle we'd managed to stay in Vegas as long as we had without them finding us—although maybe the recklessness of returning to a previous location had worked out in our favor. They probably assumed we were smarter than that.

Resting the blueprints on my lap, I closed my eyes for a moment. *Jesus. I can't remember what it was like* not *be on the run.*

Doctor Shepherd had always counseled me to take things day by day while I was at Strand, but I'd made plans for the future in my head anyway. I had daydreamed nonstop about the time when I'd finally leave the confining walls and make a normal life for myself.

But since my breakout from Strand, I'd been forced to truly follow his advice. My life had been broken down into a series of individual moments, with the unknown future stretching out in front of me like an abyss. Nothing was clear, nothing particularly mattered, beyond living through the current day, the current minute.

I wanted more than that. I wanted to think of the future again. To imagine my life with the four men who had become my mates—to hope and plan and daydream. But when I tried to picture my future with them now, all I saw was a vast, empty abyss that revealed nothing.

As if that future didn't exist.

A wave of fear washed over me at the thought, and I wrapped my arm through Noah's, clinging to him as my other hand went to Jackson's knee.

They turned to look at me, then shared a glance over my head.

"You okay, Alexis?" Jackson murmured, his amber eyes flashing with concern.

The only answer to that was one I didn't want to give, so I just shook my head slightly and tightened my grip on both of them. They seemed to understand though. Both men scooted closer to me on the seat, encasing me in the warm space between them.

"Fuck yes! Finally!"

Carl's loud voice from the front made me jump, and all heads turned to him.

"What?" Rhys asked, his voice tight.

"My hacker buddy found them. Slippery bastards covered their tracks well. They've got an official, known Strand office on the west side of the city. But it looks like a shipment of supplies was accidentally sent to the underground complex instead of the main office once. They changed the order, but the invoice still has the original address." He swiped a finger across his phone with a flourish. "Gotcha, fuckers!"

A disbelieving, slightly manic smile crossed my lips.

That was it. The last piece of the puzzle. We knew where to go.

Whoops and hollers broke out among Molly and the guys. Rhys didn't join in, but I saw his hands tighten on the steering wheel, and the van lurched as it picked up speed.

CHAPTER TWENTY-ONE

We checked into a hotel just off the interstate on the outskirts of the city, about a mile away from the location of the underground complex. It was in a remote area on the east end of Salt Lake, as far away from the public Strand location as possible. Molly and Carl checked into the penthouse suite, posing as newlyweds. Unsurprisingly, he'd already had fake IDs for the two of them ready to go—I was sure with his line of work, contingency plans were second nature.

The rest of us unloaded the van before heading up to the top floor laden down with luggage. There were several bags I didn't recognize, ones that had already been in the van when we loaded up our packs in the morning. I handled them with care, certain they were full of weapons and other equipment.

West kicked the door shut behind him as soon as we were all inside the large space. There was only one bed, a massive king-sized thing set against the far wall. A small kitchenette took up one side of the space, and there was a full extra room that was set up to be a living room or office.

The lack of beds wouldn't be an issue, since only Carl and Molly would actually spend the night here. The rest of us would be breaking into Strand and, with any luck, leaving the city with Sariah in tow before the night was over.

My brain kept trying to ask what happened after that—assuming we were successful—but my mini freakout in the van had convinced me it was better not to even ponder those questions. Not right now, anyway. There would be time for that later.

I hope.

Dropping a large backpack in the corner, I set down the other bag I carried more carefully. The contents made a metalic rattle as they settled, and I crouched beside it to tug the zipper open. Several guns were stored inside, as well as what looked like bulletproof vests and an assortment of ammunition.

"The trick is gonna be *keeping* our gear," Jackson commented, coming to stand behind me and peering over my shoulder. "If we have to shift, we'll lose pretty much anything we have on us, so we'll have to be smart about who carries what."

"Oh. Right." I craned my neck to look up at him. "I hadn't really thought about that."

"Not my first rodeo." He winked at me.

I loved that he could remain so lighthearted even in the midst of such an intense, stressful operation. I had no idea how the hell he managed it; I was a nervous wreck.

Carl was already setting up what seemed like a maze of computers and cords in the adjoining room. He called out instructions to Molly as she helped him, and I had a feeling he must *really* love her to allow her to touch his babies. With three different monitors and two laptops, it looked like the command center in some kind of spy movie.

How the hell was this real life?

"Hey, you guys need any help in there?" Jackson asked, leaning to the side to see through the door better. Carl muttered something unintelligible, waving a hand toward us. A second later, he flicked on his computers, and the light from the screens bathed his face in an eerie glow. My mate turned back to me with a grin on his face. "Ah, he's fine."

The blueprints, as it turned out, had been an even greater gift of luck than we'd realized. Not only had they given us an idea what we'd be walking into, they'd also shown us a way in. Combined with the city records Carl had accessed, we were almost certain we'd found a way in that wouldn't be guarded or rigged with an alarm.

Mainly because it wasn't an actual door.

"You should get some rest. None of us got much sleep, and it's gonna be a long night," Noah put in, coming up to stand beside Jackson as Rhys unpacked the rest of the gear Carl had procured for us.

"Are *you* going to rest?" I narrowed my eyes at him. He glanced sideways guiltily, and I shook my head. "No way then. Not unless you do."

"Damn, dude. She's got your number." Jackson chuckled.

I pointed a finger at him. "Hey, same goes for you,

buddy."

He grinned brightly at me. "If agreeing to a nap means I get to cuddle with you, then hell yeah. Count me in."

A blush warmed my cheeks, although his suggestion didn't sound half bad.

"We should all get some sleep." West strode over, addressing the two men behind me before his gaze flicked down to me briefly. "We've got our plan laid out. Once Carl's set up, he'll hack into the city's CCTV and get eyes on the Strand complex and surrounding area. Other than that, there's not much we can do till tonight."

"Then why the hell did we leave Vegas at such an ungodly fucking hour?" Jackson grumbled jokingly.

"We needed to get out of town—and we didn't know how long it would take us to find Strand. We caught a lucky break." West grinned at him, his dimples flashing. "You should *thank* me, really. Rhys wanted to get up at four a.m. I talked him down to six."

"Jesus." Jackson rolled his eyes. Then he reached down and tugged me to my feet. "Come on, Alexis. Sleep now. Insane rescue mission later."

The Strand complex was dark and quiet, the hallways empty. My bare feet slapped quietly on the polished floor, the only sound to break the silence.

The hospital gown I wore shifted gently around my body as I walked down the corridor.

No... This wasn't right. I was missing something.

The guns. The weapons. The bulletproof vest. I hadn't worn any of it—hadn't even put on shoes or clothes. How was I supposed to rescue anyone like this?

Suddenly, all the lights flashed on, bathing me in a warm, yellow glow. My heart jerked in my chest, and I spun, my heels squeaking on the floor. Doctor Shepherd stood at the end of the hall behind me, only thirty yards away. He wore his white lab coat, and his short ash-brown hair gleamed in the light.

"Alexis." His voice was soft and smooth like always. Eerily calm. "I knew you'd come back to us. This is where you belong, after all."

His thin lips tilted up into a satisfied smile as he raised the gun in his hand. He aimed it at my chest and fired.

A red-feathered dart flew straight and true, penetrating muscle and bone as it buried itself in my chest, piercing my heart. Pain exploded through me, and I collapsed to my knees, toppling sideways as my body began to seize and jerk. My head slammed against the hard floor, making my vision swim, and Doctor Shepherd's black, hard-soled shoes clipped out a steady rhythm as he strode toward me.

No. Please, no... Not like this.

"Scrubs! Scrubs!"

"Lexi!"

Hands grabbed my upper arms, holding me still as I thrashed. I opened my mouth to scream, but when my eyes flew open, piercing blue ones gazed back at me.

Not Doctor Shepherd's.

Rhys.

I let out the breath I'd pulled in on a shuddering exhale, my body finally going limp in his arms. Behind him, three other concerned faces peered down at me.

"Nightmare?" Jackson asked, wrinkling his nose sympathetically.

I nodded, blinking away the tears that stung my eyes. My heart still thudded painfully hard in my chest, and unspent adrenaline buzzed uselessly through my veins.

After hammering out the last few details of our plan, we'd all crawled onto the massive bed to rest for a few hours. I'd been convinced it was a hopeless endeavor, but surrounded on all sides by the warm bodies of my mates, soothed by the sounds of their breathing, I'd drifted off to sleep quickly.

Now I sort of wished I hadn't.

I sat up, pushing my sweat-dampened hair back from my face. "Did I wake you all up? I'm sorry. What time is it?"

The room was dim, and a soft orange light spilled under the closed door that led to the attached room.

"Eh, it's fine. We need to get up and get ready anyway. It's ten forty-five."

Jackson pressed a kiss to my forehead before sliding off the bed. Noah cupped my cheek, staring into my eyes with a probing gaze for a moment, then followed his pack mate. West looked like he wanted to say something, but he just swallowed hard and turned away.

Rhys pressed his lips into a thin line, his assessing, ice-blue gaze cutting into me. "Lexi, you don't have to come. Truly. You've done more than you realize already."

"No!" I scrambled onto my knees, ready to bolt for the

door if they tried to leave without me. "I do! And I am. I'm a part of this now, Rhys. I have to see it through! You can't—"

He stopped my tirade by pulling me toward him, his strong hands grasping my hips firmly. Then he kissed me, hard. Instinctively, my arms latched onto him, and I gave back as good as I got, my lips moving against his with a desperate fervor. When he finally broke away, I felt a little lightheaded.

His forehead rested against mine, his eyes closed and his lips so close to mine I could feel his breath on my skin. "Of course I want you there. I want you by my side. Always."

A starburst of emotions exploded inside my chest at his declaration, and I clung to him for a few seconds longer, needing to prolong this moment, to lock it away tight somewhere I could never lose it.

I was terrified of what might happen tonight—that one or more of us might not survive to see the dawn. But we were in this together, and I wouldn't change that for the world.

"You have me, Rhys," I whispered. "For as long as I li—"

His lips met mine again, cutting off my words with a single kiss.

"*Forever*, Lexi," he murmured, his voice rough. "I won't take anything less."

When he looked down at me, I could see all my own fears reflected back in his eyes. But I saw hope there too. And so much love and determination, it nearly overwhelmed me.

"Forever." I echoed his words then tightened my arms around him, drawing in a deep breath. "But first, let's go get your sister."

CHAPTER TWENTY-TWO

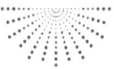

My breath fogged the air in front of my face, and I rubbed my hands up and down my arms, grateful that our operation had required us all to wear long-sleeved, black tactical wear. It was early summer, but it still cooled down a lot at night.

West peered around the side of the building we hid behind, scoping out the single story structure across the street. It too, was similar to the Strand complex outside of Austin. Just like that one, this building seemed designed to deflect attention, to let the eye slide right over it and the casual observer immediately forget about it.

He pulled his head back, nodding at us. "I see the path around the side Carl told us about. There's a front entrance, and an employee entrance around back." Then he pressed a hand to his ear, speaking into the small communication device Carl had given him. "Carl, you got the cameras taken out?"

I couldn't hear the other man's response, but West nodded, satisfied with whatever answer he received. Only he and Rhys wore the devices, and they'd try not to shift unless absolutely necessary, so we could maintain a connection to our outside eye.

"He's got the cameras turned off, and he's watching all the streets in a three block radius. If unexpected company arrives, he'll be able to give us a heads up," Rhys reported.

I fingered the gun holstered to my belt, trying to find comfort in the cold steel. My wolf whined inside me, anxious to get this fucking waiting over with and do *something*.

West glanced up and down the street to make sure the coast was clear, then gestured us forward with two fingers. We darted down the empty sidewalk like shadows, heading away from Strand's dummy building. As innocuous as the front door looked, there was no way the entrances weren't rigged with state-of-the-art alarms. Trying to break in that way would be nearly impossible and way too risky.

When the men had broken into the complex where they found me, they'd used their man on the inside—Noah, or *Cliff,* as I'd thought he was called then—to get them into the building. But we didn't have time to send an undercover agent in this time; and it would've been impossible anyway. Strand wouldn't fall for the same trick again.

That left us having to break in the old-fashioned way.

Several blocks away, when the single-story brick building was no longer in sight, West slowed, veering into the street. Noah stepped up beside him, and the two men bent to slide a manhole cover out of place. The rest of us joined them, crouching around the small, dark hole in the middle of the pavement.

"Fuck. Are we sure this is a good idea?" Jackson made a face in the darkness.

"No." West snorted. "But it's the best option we had out of a pile of shitty ones."

"Oh, right. That."

Rhys pulled a small flashlight from his tactical vest, shining it down the hole. "Come on. We gotta hurry."

He slipped inside the open hole, his feet finding the rusty iron bars that formed a ladder along one side. He clamped the flashlight between his teeth, the small circle of light illuminating the rough brick of the wall as he descended quickly. I followed after him before I could lose my nerve, and Noah came after me.

About twenty-five feet down, the claustrophobic brick chute opened up into a wider space. I climbed down several more steps before my boots landed on solid ground, and I moved away to make room for the others. It was pitch black in the tunnel, the kind of darkness that swallowed up light, that seemed to have a form and shape all its own. Rhys's little flashlight barely penetrated the gloom, and I tried to tamp down the goose bumps that rose along my skin.

"This way." He reached out to squeeze my hand once before starting down the wide, dank tunnel.

It was larger than I would've imagined, with ceilings at least twelve feet high and stained cement walls. My sense of direction wasn't good, but I'd memorized the path we needed to take, just in case. As intersecting tunnels met with ours, we turned left, then right, then right again. The guys crowded around me, all of us sticking close together, but not even the warmth from their bodies could dispel the damp chill in the air.

Finally, West held a hand up, bringing us to a stop.

Rhys swept the beam of his flashlight around, pausing on a dark metal grate that sat high on the wall. "There. Just like Carl said."

Without hesitation, West and Noah stepped toward the wall, gripping each other's forearms to create a makeshift platform. Jackson pulled the blowtorch and a pair of goggles out of the bag slung over his back, tossing the empty sack on the ground. He slipped the goggles on then stepped onto his pack mates' linked arms, and they raised him up as he braced one hand against the wall to keep himself steady. When he was level with the grate, he flipped the blowtorch on.

"Avert your eyes," he commanded in a mock-solemn tone, but he didn't need to tell me twice. The flame burned so bright it made the surrounding darkness seem thicker somehow, and when I blinked, little white spots danced in my vision. I kept my eyes turned away, counting down the minutes impatiently until the soft whoosh of the blowtorch died out and there was a clanging sound.

"Sorry. Sorry." Jackson grunted. "It's open."

Excitement stirred in my belly as I stepped forward, peering up at the newly-made opening in the side of the wall. Rhys's dim beam shone on it like a spotlight as Jackson reached up and hauled himself through the hole.

I followed, panic flaring for a moment at the possibility

that I'd be too short to reach the damn thing. But I'd forgotten I was teamed up with four massive, muscled shifters. Noah and West lifted me so quickly I was practically launched up the side of the wall, and Jackson caught my wrists, pulling me through into the metal duct.

He scooted backward to make room for me, before calling over my shoulder in a low voice, "You guys good?"

"Yeah. Go on ahead. But once you get out of the duct, *wait for us.*"

There was a subtle note of warning in West's voice, but he needn't have worried. Jackson might set vans on fire for fun, but when it came to shit like this, he wouldn't act reckless or impulsive. It was too important.

"So far, so good," Jackson murmured, shooting me a small smile as he urged me forward.

We crawled through the ducts, moving slowly to remain as quiet as possible. According to the building's blueprints, there were five levels to the Strand complex, not counting the single story that sat above ground. If our estimations were correct, the air vent leading from the tunnel would spit us out on the third level. Based on the layout of the only other complex we knew of, it seemed unlikely that the test subjects would be kept too close to the surface, so we'd go down before working our way back up.

We reached a painted grate at the end of the tight tunnel, and Jackson drew a few tools from his vest, squeezing past me to unscrew it before pulling it into the duct. Then he dropped to the floor below before reaching up to help me down. The rest of my mates crawled out behind us, landing lightly on booted feet.

"They've got sensor beams set up across the doorways. Look." Jackson jerked his head toward a door a little way down the hall. Two thin blue lines of light crossed the frame.

"They're spaced pretty far apart. We should be able to get through without tripping the alarms," West murmured.

"Yeah. Just be careful," Noah added.

I swiveled my gaze up and down the long corridor. It had white walls and a tiled floor, and something about it was so intimately familiar that my heartbeat faltered. My wolf whined as the nightmare I'd had rushed through my mind again, and I wondered if it really *had* been a huge mistake to come here.

"Jesus. This place is creepy as fuck," Jackson whispered beside me.

"Brings back memories, doesn't it?" Noah asked.

"Yeah." Rhys's voice was hard, edged with soul-biting anger. "But nothing I ever wanted to relive."

Hearing the agitation in their voices actually soothed my raw nerves a little. This was hard for all of us. It didn't make me weak to not want to be here. It made me sane.

West pulled out a second flashlight, its beam bouncing off the sterile walls as we crept down the darkened corridors. Every time we passed through a doorway, we had to maneuver carefully between the blue beams of light, making my palms sweat and my heart clench. If a single beam was broken, all of Strand would know we were here.

We did a thorough sweep of the entire floor, passing

offices and storage rooms, but saw no sign of any living creatures.

"Let's try the next level down," Noah murmured as we passed through the large open space that formed the central hub.

"Carl? Third level is clear." West spoke into the earpiece he wore, nodding at the response that came through. He glanced over his shoulder at the rest of us. "Next floor down has the small holding areas. Below that are the large rooms."

My mouth was dry as sandpaper, so I didn't even try to speak. I just nodded in agreement, and the five of us veered down another hallway toward a new set of stairs.

The next level down was unlike anything I'd seen at the Austin Strand complex—it looked more like something out of my nightmares. The wide area that made up the main hub had large metal cages lining the walls. Everything looked dingier and more worn down, and a lingering smell—like wet fur—pervaded the air. Scratch marks marred the linoleum tiles.

Rhys and West moved around the perimeter, placing small devices that looked like silly-putty with wires sticking out of them in the corners of the room. My reluctant feet dragged me toward one of the cages. It was about six feet tall by ten feet wide, and a dog bowl sat inside, half-full of water. My stomach twisted as I imagined some hapless shifter stuck in here, treated no better than a wild animal, and anger burned hot in my chest.

"What is this place?" I whispered, the sound choked and rough.

"Training area." Jackson spat the words, his amber eyes blazing in the dim light. "It was never enough for Strand to just create shifters. They want to see what their little toys can do, what different test subjects are capable of."

"So they... train the shifters?"

"They try. But we're not fucking dogs—something Doctor Shepherd and his team of monsters never quite seemed to realize."

I shivered. What must life have been like for Sariah all these years? Assuming she was truly in this compound, what had she been forced to undergo in the name of research?

Rhys stalked up beside me, hands clenched into fists. His nostrils flared, and I knew it was taking all his willpower not to pummel the metal cage with his fists and boots. But unleashing his rage wouldn't help get Sariah back. And we were so close.

I rested a hand on his shoulder. His whole body was shaking, his muscles straining like rubber bands pulled taut.

"We'll get Sariah out of here, Rhys," I whispered. "Let's keep going."

He jerked his head in a stiff nod, but I felt him release the breath he'd been holding. He turned to join West, and the two of them led us toward another hallway, pausing to slip between the blue beams that criss-crossed the hall's entrance. Large glass windows lined the walls, revealing the interiors of the small rooms we'd seen on the blueprints. From time to time, one of the men would deposit another of the small devices Carl had given us.

Some rooms had examining tables like the ones I'd sat on

for countless visits and checkups. Some had hospital beds. Some had cots set against the walls.

Trying to close my mind off to the horrific images it kept conjuring up, I quickened my pace, stepping quietly behind West and Rhys.

A sudden loud *thud* came from my right, and I yelped, scrambling away from the sound. My heart crashed against my ribs as the four men around me all turned toward the noise, braced for a fight.

My breath caught in my throat.

A face pressed against the glass of the room next to us. Two bony-fingered hands splayed across the pane, leaving streaks of grime and sweat as they dragged over the smooth surface.

It was a woman. Maybe in her early thirties, with stringy blond hair and wild eyes.

"*Get out!*"

Her voice was muffled by the thick glass, but it was easy to hear the panic and fear it held.

"Holy fuck," Jackson muttered, his eyes wide.

The woman's body jerked, her bones morphing and stretching beneath her skin. But she didn't shift. She grimaced in pain, pressing herself against the glass as though she could force her way through it. After a moment, her bones settled, leaving her still in human form.

She gasped for breath, her head shaking back and forth as tears streamed down her cheeks. Then she slapped the glass again, hard, making me jump.

"Get out!" she screeched. "*Get out get out get out!*"

I couldn't catch my breath. Fear, revulsion, and pity all struggled for dominance inside me, and the resulting mess of emotions made me feel like throwing up. "What... what's wrong with her?"

"She can't shift." West's jaw muscles pulsed. Soft blue light glowed from a bank of monitors on the wall inside the room, spilling into the hallway and giving the woman's gaunt face a ghostly sheen. "She's stuck halfway. Her body keeps breaking apart and reforming on the inside."

Oh, fuck. I tried to imagine the pain I experienced during a shift tearing through my body over and over, and blanched at the chill that washed over me.

"They *still* haven't perfected it," Jackson muttered, his lip curling. "When will they fucking give up and stop trying to play God?"

The woman had her forehead pressed against the glass again, her face contorted in an agonized expression as she stared at us. Her fingers curled convulsively like dying spiders, and her chest rose and fell with deep, ragged breaths.

I inched away as Jackson stepped forward, ducking his head to meet the woman's gaze. He shook his head sadly, reaching a hand up to press against hers through the glass.

Just as his palm touched the window, an earsplitting alarm broke the silence, blasting through the deserted corridor like a hurricane.

I froze, suspended in place by the sound as fear thickened my blood.

He yanked his hand back, whipping around to face us. "Shit! I didn't do anything. I swear!"

CHAPTER TWENTY-THREE

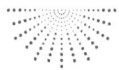

"What the fuck happened?" Jackson looked stricken. "Was it the glass? How the fuck—?"

The earsplitting siren drilled into my skull as we all cast around wildly, searching for the source of the threat. Noah's gaze fell on me, and the expression on his face made my blood run cold.

I glanced down.

The thin blue line of light running across the doorframe behind me had been intersected by the back of my leg. Just barely. But enough.

Disbelief and shock twisted my stomach, and I stepped forward quickly. But the alarm didn't stop. I had tripped the sensor, and I couldn't undo that.

"Carl! Can you—" West cupped a hand over his ear, struggling to hear something on the other end. Then he looked up, his expression grim. "The sensors were triggered and tripped the alarm. Carl picked up the signal."

"Shit." Noah ran a hand through his hair. "How long do we have?"

"Not long. Carl's checking cameras in a larger radius, and he'll give us as much warning as possible. But given the response time at the Austin complex, I'd guess less than ten minutes."

"Fuck. *Fuck!*" Rhys tilted his head back and roared, the sound barely rising above the blare of the alarm. He drew a gun from the holster at his side, jerking his head in our direction. "Go! Get out now. I'm going after Sariah."

"Are you fucking crazy, man?" Jackson's eyes widened in disbelief.

"I'm not getting this close again and leaving without her!" Rhys insisted. "If we fail, who knows what the fuck they'll do to everyone left in this place? They could kill all the subjects here just to keep their secret safe! I'm not—"

"No, I meant you're fucking crazy if you think we're leaving you behind, you asshole!" Jackson shouted over the alarm, shaking his head like Rhys was an idiot. "We don't abandon our own."

The other two men nodded, and I felt my head bobble on my neck. Fear coursed through me like liquid metal, so strong my knees practically knocked together. But this had been my fault. *I* had tripped the alarm, sent the call out to the hunters, and there was no way I could abandon Rhys to face them alone.

And he was right. This was our last chance.

After this, there would be no more options.

Rhys's face contorted in a grimace, and he seemed to be

wrestling with his instinct to force us all to leave, to keep us safe. But there wasn't time to argue, and he knew it.

He nodded once, his bright blue eyes flashing.

Then he turned toward the window, raising his gun. The woman's eyes widened in understanding. She stepped back just before he fired two shots into the left side of the large pane. The glass shattered as the half-shifter inside the room let out a yowl. Her body rippled painfully again, but she shuffled forward through the shards of glass. She didn't have to be a full wolf to sense freedom when it beckoned.

Holstering his weapon, Rhys strode forward, reaching through the now-open frame and grabbing the woman by the arms. His body was tense, but his voice was surprisingly gentle as he spoke to her.

"Hey, hey! It's okay. You're okay. What's your name?"

The woman blinked up at him with a blank expression for a moment, like she couldn't quite understand the question. Then she muttered, "J—Julie."

"Hi, Julie. I'm Rhys. We'll get you out of here, all right?" He ducked his head, trying to catch and hold her wild gaze. "But we need you to help us. Are there others here? Where are they?"

The woman's mouth opened and closed a few times before she forced the words out. "Yes. D—downstairs. I can... show you."

Leaning farther inside the room, Rhys scooped the woman up. She was so thin and frail he lifted her easily, helping her out of the small room. She wore a hospital gown, and her bare legs stuck out from the oversized garment like two pale sticks. When he set her down in the hallway, she almost collapsed again as another partial shift wracked her body.

He steadied her, and she clung to his vest, gasping for air. When the wave passed, she looked up, her eyes a little more focused.

"Downstairs. Come."

Julie hobbled down the hallway, most of her weight supported by Rhys. Jackson darted up on her other side, slipping an arm around her too.

Even through my fear, my heart swelled with love for these men. Strand had destroyed my faith in people, but these four shifters had managed to revive it, slowly but surely.

They *needed* to live. The world couldn't afford to lose them. And neither could I.

"Come on, Scrubs."

Noah's hand slid into mine, jerking me out of my frozen state. I gripped it hard as we dashed down the hallway after the others. Julie led us to another set of stairs hidden behind a locked door, and without missing a beat, Rhys shot out the lock. There was no point in subtlety now—we just needed to be fast.

We hustled down the steps, the metal stairs shaking under our pounding footsteps, and burst through another door into the lowest level of the complex.

The "wet fur" smell was worse down here. I could feel my wolf twitching inside me as we raced down a short, wide hallway. The scent agitated her.

"There. Through there!"

The half-shifter woman's voice was rough, as if she'd shredded her vocal cords screaming. I could barely hear it over the nonstop blare of the alarm. But she was moving more steadily now, seeming to draw strength from her new mission.

West shot out the lock on the double doors and kicked them apart, sending them flying open. The space beyond was dark and open—one of the huge rooms we'd seen on the blueprints. He swept his flashlight around in a quick sweep, and my gaze followed the beam.

Scattered around the large space, which was about the size of the training yard in the Strand complex where I'd grown up, were shadowy forms. He held his light steady on one, and I gasped when the keen eyes of a wolf snapped toward us. The animal leapt to its feet, hackles rising. All around us, I could sense movement as other shifters roused themselves.

"Sariah? Sariah!!" Rhys bellowed into the darkness, his booming voice rising over the alarm. He turned on his own flashlight, leaving Jackson to support the frail woman beside him as he spun in a circle, illuminating more shifters—some in human form, some wolf.

"*Rhys!*"

The breathy scream caught my ear a second before a willowy girl flew across the room, hurling herself into Rhys's arms. The flashlight dropped from his hand, skittering across the floor, but in the ambient light from the beam, I could see him wrap his arms around the girl, holding her tight. She was naked, but her long black hair fell nearly to her hips.

Sariah.

She was here. We'd found her.

She and Rhys clung to each other as if their lives depended on it, ignoring the world around them for the moment, but West and Noah turned to the other shifters.

"We're getting out of here," West said loudly. "We came for her, but you can all come with us if you want."

The words seemed to snap Rhys out of his bubble, and he broke away from Sariah, his expression hardening. We still had to get out of here, or their reunion would be for nothing.

"Trust them!" Sariah called, turning to face the others, her hand gripping Rhys's. "This... this is my brother. He's a shifter."

"Guys, we gotta go!" Jackson shot an anxious glance toward the door, bouncing on his feet. "Like, *yesterday!*"

West reached a hand up, cupping it over his ear, and Rhys mimicked the gesture. Their expressions shifted at the exact same time, and their eyes locked.

"Damn it. We're out of fucking time. They're here."

Rhys's voice was low, but I heard him anyway. Whatever hunters had been called by the alarm had arrived. And we were stuck on the lowest level of the underground complex. All they had to do to end us was box us in.

"Is there another way up besides the way we came down?" Jackson grabbed the half-shifter's shoulders, biting his lip as he searched her face desperately. Behind him, West dashed to the corners of the room, placing several charges on the floor.

Julie shuddered as her body tried to shift, panting when

she answered. "There are two... other rooms... like this. Empty. Stairs lead down to each one."

"Can you take us?"

She nodded jerkily. I bent to pick up Rhys's discarded flashlight, sweeping it over the shifters that followed us as we headed for the door. Some were in decent shape, but some looked almost as malnourished as Julie did. These test subjects obviously hadn't been cared for the same way I had been.

Because I was *special*.

Anger and disgust burned through me as Julie guided us through a series of smaller hallways. When we hit another wide corridor, she jerked her head toward the door at the end. We passed through it and pounded up the steps, our noise level increasing exponentially now that our group had more than tripled in size. Several of the shifters remained in wolf form, their massive forms moving quickly.

We made it up two flights before the stairs stopped, bunching us up in a traffic jam of fur and bodies. This was the same level we'd emerged on originally; if my sense of direction was right at all, we were at the end of one of the spokes. We'd need to go farther in toward the main hub to find the stairs that led all the way to the surface.

Jackson nudged the door open, peering into the hall, then nodded and stepped out. Julie no longer clung to him for support, although her body still shuddered with repressed shifts. Her teeth were clenched in a grimace, but the adrenaline surging through her system appeared to be lending her strength.

She also didn't seem to know her way around this level, so Jackson took the lead, hustling down the dark hallway toward the open doorway into the main hub.

We were halfway there when the siren stopped.

The sudden silence in the air was so jarring that I almost tripped over my own feet, stumbling until West caught me with a grip on my arm.

Then the lights went on, the overhead fluorescents banishing the dark shadows around us. I gasped, nearly blinded by the sudden change.

I hadn't considered the darkness all that comforting, but the light was terrifying. My footsteps slowed, my gaze riveted to the opening at the end of the hall.

"Don't stop!"

Jackson put on an extra burst of speed, the hard soles of his boots pounding on the floor as he reached out to Julie to pull her along.

My heart felt like it was trying to crawl up my throat, and I gasped for air as fear stole my breath. A stitch jabbed my side, but I ignored it, sprinting full out down the blindingly bright hallway.

Finally, we spilled out into the large open space in the middle. It was so much more civilized than the matching room one level below. No cages lined the walls here, no claw marks scored the tile. This level was for humans, not the animals they tried to tame.

Jackson slowed, swiveling his head around as he searched for a viable exit. He veered to the left, leading us toward another corridor that led away from the main room.

But before we reached it, several burly men in tactical gear stepped forward to fill the space.

"Aw, shit!"

He skidded, changing direction. But it was too late. Strand hunters stood in every doorway leading out of this room, except the one we'd just come through—and we already knew that led to a dead end.

Jackson pulled up short in the center of the large space, and I stumbled to a stop, colliding with West and Noah as they pressed close to me, guns drawn. Humans murmured and wolves snarled as the group of shifters we'd freed gathered in a tight knot around us.

No. Not freed.

We were nowhere close to free yet.

CHAPTER TWENTY-FOUR

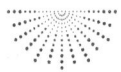

Everyone stood frozen for a heartbeat, and my gaze darted around the space. There were at least fifty hunters gathered around us, filling up the entryways and boxing us in. All the men threatening us were big, muscled, and carried themselves like soldiers. But the face I dreaded most—the chiseled features, thick neck, and short spiked hair of the blond Terminator, Nils—wasn't present.

Good. At least I wouldn't be killed by that fucker.

"Take the subject in the middle alive. Keep one or two of the other intruders alive for questioning," a man with short red hair barked. "Put down any others you have to."

The other hunters nodded sharply. As if they shared a single brain, all of them stepped forward, closing in on us. The wolves around me shifted and growled, hackles rising. Sariah, still in human form, tried to step in front of Rhys, but he stuck an arm out, holding her back. His other hand held a gun aimed at the hunters.

For a moment, tension crackled in the air like lightning. Then one of the shifter wolves lunged forward, teeth snapping. A dark-haired hunter swiveled to the right, about to take the wolf down—but before he could shoot, Rhys's gun let off a quick *pop-pop*. The hunter went down with a cry, one arm flying up to clutch at the bullet wounds in his shoulder. Without missing a beat, the wolf leapt on him, tearing into the man's wounded shoulder as if she were trying to remove the bullets with her teeth.

The man screamed, and chaos erupted.

More gunshots fired from the hunters surrounding us, and our tight group broke apart as people scrambled for cover. The room was mostly bare, so there wasn't much to hide behind. I ducked, clutching the grip of my own weapon with sweaty hands. Snarls and yells rose in the air around me, punctuated by the loud bangs of gunfire.

Beside me, West glanced around wildly. "We need to get out of this room! We're sitting ducks in he—"

His words were cut off with a grunt as a bullet slammed into his chest. Surprise and pain registered on his face as he went down, his body propelled backward by the force of the blow. He hit the floor hard, and time seemed to stop.

My *heart* stopped.

A piece of my soul withered and died.

No... Not West. Not my mate.

Rhys roared, stepping forward to aim at the man who'd taken down West. One shot ended his life, but I didn't celebrate the hunter's death. I hardly noticed the blood.

My attention was riveted to West's chest, as Rhys covered

us and Jackson scrambled over to him, running his hands over the dark vest he wore. After a second, West coughed, rolling over onto his side as he gasped for air.

"Fuck. He's okay! The vest stopped the bullet." Jackson looked up, his amber eyes shining with relief.

My blood turned to water in my veins. Even hearing those words wasn't enough to banish the cold fear that ran through me at the thought of what could've happened. How much worse it could've been.

My wolf howled at the devastating vision, rage filling her —filling me. Her anger was my anger as I spun, setting my sights on a pair of hunters who'd taken cover in the doorway and were shooting into the room.

With a feral scream, I ran toward them, aiming my weapon and squeezing the trigger over and over, just like West had instructed me to the first time he'd put a gun in my hands.

I was a lousy fucking shot, and every single bullet I fired missed its target. But it didn't matter. It kept them from attacking anyone else, kept them from shooting at me. When I was just a few yards away, I tossed my gun to the floor, letting the shift that had been burning inside me finally happen. Even as I continued forward, my muscles and bones broke apart and reformed, fur sprouting and snout elongating. Teeth and claws growing.

It hurt like it always did, but the sharp bite of pain only fed my rage, spurring me on. As soon as I was fully wolf, I leapt, pushing off the slick, tiled floor with my massive back paws.

I saw the men's expressions change. The two large hunters, schooled in combat and violence, blanched with fear at the sight of me. Both of them raised their weapons, but by the time they did, I was already on them. I hit one with the full force of my weight, bowling him over. One bite took care of his shooting arm. Another snap of my jaws ended his life.

While I was distracted, the other man leapt on top of me, wrapping his arm around my neck and digging the barrel of his gun into my fur. I howled, shaking like a wet dog, but he clung fiercely.

"Scrubs!"

Noah's voice was laced with panic, and a second later, a gunshot pierced the air. A sting of pain snapped at my side, and for a moment, I thought that was it— the hunter had shot me.

I waited for the world to go black as death claimed me. But instead, the man on top of me groaned.

Liquid dripped onto my fur as his muscles slackened, his weight seeming to increase as he went limp. I shook again, and he slid off me, falling onto his back on the floor. He'd been shot through the chest—the same bullet must've hit me too, but had barely done any damage.

I shot a glance at Noah, my enhanced sight picking up every detail of his features as relief and worry moved across his face. His gun was still aimed at the man.

There was no time to thank him though. Movement in my periphery drew my attention, and I whirled just as two more hunters raced toward me. Blood dripped from my muzzle as I drew my lips back in a warning snarl. I threw myself at the first man, tearing through his flesh like tissue paper. I clamped my jaws around his arm and yanked, throwing him off balance. Then I turned for the next man, hungry for more, desperate to sate my predatory rage. His blood tasted like copper on my tongue, mingling with the sweeter taste of the first hunter's.

Shouts, screams, and howls became my soundtrack as I moved without thought, letting the wild savagery of my wolf reign. I attacked like a machine, tearing through flesh and bone over and over again.

Finally, words pierced the battle haze in my skull.

"Alexis! We gotta go! You've cleared an exit. We need to get the fuck outta here!"

Jackson stood in the doorway where the hunters had been taking cover, his arm still draped around Julie. She looked worse, sagging in his grip as her muscles and bones moved under her skin—as if she'd already burned through every bit of strength the adrenaline had given her.

My mate aimed into the room, firing occasionally at anyone who got too close. Inside the large space, several downed wolf bodies lay on the unforgiving tile, joining the bodies of the dead hunters.

Pain stabbed my heart. *Damn it.* We'd tried to rescue all the prisoners in this complex, but if we didn't get the fuck out of here soon, our appearance would end up being their death sentence instead.

I dipped my large head, my tongue darting out to lap at the blood that covered my nose and muzzle. Then I glanced behind me. The arched, open doorway where Jackson stood led to a corridor. I barely recognized it with the lights on, but I could tell by the scent it was the same one we'd come down when we'd first emerged from the vent.

Tilting my head back, I howled, the urgent, plaintive sound drawing the attention of the other shifters in the room. Rhys and West barreled toward me, Sariah sandwiched between them. Something in my heart unwound a little to see West back on his feet, but bloodlust was pounding too hard in my veins for a proper celebration.

The other wolves and shifters raced toward us as we sped down the hall toward a stairwell access door.

"Go! Go, go!" Jackson gestured them through, holding the door as Rhys and West laid down cover fire for them. Noah had shifted sometime during the fight, and his muzzle glistened with blood as he urged the stragglers on. Julie sagged against the wall, her eyelids drooping.

When the last of the shifter test subjects was through the door, Rhys jerked his head, and the rest of us darted through after them. Our footsteps sounded like rolling thunder as we raced up the stairs, moving as quickly as we could in such a confined space. As we reached the landing of the next level, the stairwell door below us opened again.

Shit. They were right on top of us.

"Faster! Fucking faster!"

Jackson had his arm wrapped around Julie's waist, practically carrying her up the stairs like a sack of potatoes, and I had a sudden sense of déjà vu as the memory of our first escape from Strand washed over me. Of the men helping me stay on my feet as I stumbled, my limbs numb from shock and fear.

Panting and gasping, we rounded the corner of the next flight of stairs.

So close.

But so many of us jostling together slowed us down. I glanced back. The hunter leading our pursuers—the burly red-headed man who'd called out instructions—whipped around the corner behind us, bracing his feet on the landing as he aimed his gun, steadying the grip with both hands.

"*No!*" Julie's voice was little more than a croak, but she tore herself away from Jackson's grip.

Her shifting features contorted in a mask of rage as she turned to face the hunter, running back toward him. Broken, unstable limbs propelled her forward as a gunshot rang out.

The bullet hit her in the gut, but it was too late. With a ragged cry, she launched herself off the landing, flying down the stairs toward the man, gravity turning her into a half-human wrecking ball. He fired again before she landed on top of him, wrapping her arms and legs around him as they both went down. They fell together, tumbling down the stairs in a messy tangle of limbs. His head struck the steps at an awkward angle, and when they came to a rest on the landing below, they both lay still.

"Fuck!" Jackson stared down after them, his face a mask of shock. He moved to run down the stairs, but West caught his shoulder.

"She's gone, man. She's gone."

Jackson's wild amber eyes darted between West and the contorted bodies in the stairwell. Julie's small form was sprawled across the hunter's larger one, her limbs no longer rippling, her bones no longer breaking and reforming.

Blood spread slowly from the two bullet wounds that had taken her life, but the expression on her face was tranquil. Almost peaceful.

Her suffering was over.

But already, the door below was opening again. New pursuers would be on us any second. Wrenching his gaze away, Jackson joined West, and we sprinted up the stairs. West threw down the last of his charges as we went, no longer bothering to place them carefully. The shifter pack was ahead of us now, and by the time we finally reached a hallway on the ground floor, the last few test subjects were slipping out the employee access door at the back of building.

I put on a final burst of speed, my thick claws gouging into the floor. Jackson and Noah brought up the rear, their panting breaths reassuring me they were still there, while West and Rhys raced ahead of me. Sariah had shifted to wolf form like Noah, but still stuck close to her brother as we spilled out into the cool night air, joining the rest of the shifters.

West shot a look over his shoulder, making sure we'd all cleared the door, then turned to Rhys quickly. "Light it up, brother. Now!"

"With fucking pleasure."

Pushing his dark hair out of his face, Rhys pulled the detonator Carl had given him from his pocket. His gaze flicked to Sariah for a half-second, a look of fierce protectiveness overtaking his face.

Then he flipped the top off and jammed his thumb on the button.

CHAPTER TWENTY-FIVE

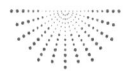

For a moment, nothing happened.

My heart skipped a beat. Would it fail? Had we placed the explosives wrong? Maybe they were too far away to be detonated remotely.

Then a faint noise caught my ear, almost more of a feeling than a sound.

The first explosions were so far below ground they barely registered. But after a few seconds, deep, louder booms could be heard. Then several more sounded, growing in intensity.

Finally, a fireball burst through the employee access door we'd just come through, spitting out a burning figure with it. The man screamed and writhed, throwing himself to the ground and rolling to put out the flames that licked across his skin. Before he could even stand, several wolves pounced on him, ending his life in a harsh cry.

Silence fell, the peaceful sound so strange and eerie it made my skin prickle, putting my hackles on end. No more figures emerged from the building. No sirens or alarms cut the air.

The explosions had grown loud enough to be heard even above ground, but at this hour of the night in this remote corner of Salt Lake City, no one was around to hear it.

But we couldn't count on that luck to hold for long. What had been a group of five going in was now nearly thirty, with a mix of clothed and naked humans and large wolves. There was absolutely nothing subtle about us.

"Carl?" West turned his head, speaking into his earpiece. "We're out. And... we've got a few more people with us than we expected. Any other company on the way?"

He listened intently, then shook his head at us. I whuffed out a relieved breath, and Noah's wolf nuzzled my neck.

Rhys spoke up, addressing Carl too. "Can you redirect surveillance cameras to give us a clear path out of town? We need to get into the foothills. I don't know how long we have before they send reinforcements."

Whatever Carl said must've been something like "yes," because Rhys jerked his head, gesturing for us to follow him.

Sariah shifted back to her human form then turned to the others, her blue eyes—such a close match to Rhys's—shining. Her voice shook slightly, but she was keeping her shit together way better than I had after my rescue. "We're not safe yet. You don't have to come with us if you don't want, but I'm sticking with my brother. I'm *not* getting caught again."

Rhys shot her a proud look before grabbing her hand and leading us away from the building. The other shifters must've shared Sariah's sentiment about not getting caught again, because every single one of them followed. Those still in human form had glassy eyes and dazed expressions, and several of the wolves limped or nursed injuries.

Shit. They were in rough shape—physically and emotionally. We needed to get somewhere safe as soon as possible.

But where *was* safe?

Was any location, no matter how remote, truly secure as long as Strand was still out there? As long as they were still conducting tests? As long as they still wanted their experiments back?

I swallowed down the acidic despair that crept up my throat. I should be celebrating. We had *won*. We'd rescued Sariah and the other shifters that padded along silently behind us as Rhys guided us along the quiet back roads leading out of Salt Lake City.

We hadn't been able to save everyone, and the weight of that guilt dragged at me. But in this long and deadly game we were playing against Strand, we had to take our victories where we could find them. We'd managed to rescue almost two dozen shifter test subjects. We were still alive.

And we would do what we had to to keep surviving.

My wolf form retreated as we walked, slipping back down inside me unbidden. I honestly wasn't ready for her to let go; my human form felt puny and weak after the power of the wolf. Rocks and twigs dug into the soles of my feet, and the night air tickled my bare skin. Noah shifted beside me, wrapping his arm around my shoulders and lending me some of his strength and warmth. We were both covered with blood—a mixture of ours and the hunters'—but I couldn't bring myself to care.

My body was leaden with exhaustion as we slowly left the buildings and byways behind, making our way into the rocky terrain that surrounded the city. Finally, Rhys came to a halt on a flat stretch of earth nestled between tall rocks. They formed a makeshift barrier, protecting us on three sides, and that shelter eased the worry eating away at me a little.

If more hunters found us here, at least they couldn't surround us again.

As the rescued shifters settled anxiously into the small space, Rhys turned to his sister again. He stared down into her face with penetrating eyes that burned with love and pain, but he didn't speak. He didn't know what to say, I realized. The black-haired shifter felt so much, but he wasn't always great at expressing those emotions—at least, not until the dam broke and they poured out of him all at once in a torrent.

"Are you... all right?" he forced out roughly.

She nodded, tear tracks streaking the dirt and blood smeared across her cheeks. "You came. You came back."

"I told you I would, Sah. I promised."

Her head bobbed up and down again, and then she lurched forward, gripping him in another bone-crushing hug as she buried her face in his chest. He stroked her hair, closing his eyes as tears ran down his cheeks too. A lump rose in my throat as I watched them, and when Rhys's gaze found mine, I looked away quickly, not wanting to intrude on their private moment.

But when they finally drew back, he took Sariah's arm gently, steering her over toward me.

"Sah, this is Alexis. My mate. She helped us find you." His voice was warm with pride and love as he said the words.

Her eyes went wide as she blinked up at me. I couldn't quite read her reaction, and I wasn't sure how to greet her. I wanted to pull her into a hug, but I was a stranger, and she'd been through so much trauma, I wasn't sure that was a good idea. We were also both naked, bloody, and exhausted. Not exactly the ideal "meet the family" moment.

"Thank you," she whispered.

Before we could say anything else, West raised a hand to his ear, nodding in response to words I couldn't hear. Then he turned to face us. "Carl's on his way. He'll bring our bags and a few other things we'll need. He thinks he can help get us out of here."

Jackson and Noah joined us, and the six of us formed a small huddle.

"Where are we going?" Sariah's eyes were wide, and she kept darting her gaze back the way we'd come, as if expecting to be hauled back to the Strand compound any second. Hell, I could relate to that. I still felt that way most days, and I'd escaped over two months ago.

The men all shared a look over our heads; Sariah was taller than me, but still shorter than her brother and his pack mates.

"New York?" Jackson wrinkled his nose. "That was the original plan."

"What's in New York?" she asked.

"Nothing," Rhys grunted. "It's just far away from here. And big enough that we could disappear. But..."

He trailed off, glancing over at the cluster of shifters who'd followed us out of the Strand complex. They huddled close together, almost all of them back in wolf forms now, their eyes gleaming in the darkness as they gazed at us.

"It doesn't feel right, does it?" Noah followed his gaze.

Rhys shook his head, his expression torn.

"Will they come with us?" West asked Sariah, jerking his head toward the shifters.

Her eyebrows shot up. "To... New York? I don't know. They're not... New York is..." She made a gesture as if she was encompassing a large space.

I could relate to that too. Unlike Sariah and the other rescued shifters, I hadn't known I was being held in captivity the whole time I lived at the Strand complex outside Austin. But regardless, stepping into the outside world after years spent locked away had been completely overwhelming. Everything had felt exhilarating but terrifying. Too big, too loud—too much.

New York City might be the worst possible place to take a bunch of shell-shocked shifters.

"No, not New York." Noah chewed his lip thoughtfully, his gaze darting around the circle. "What about the Lost Pack?"

"Fucking hell," Rhys groaned. "This again?"

"It makes sense though!" Jackson piped up. "And we know exactly where they are this time. Val gave us the coordinates. The six of us can move on from there, find another place to go if we want. But there's nowhere else I can think of to take a whole complex-full of shifters."

"The Lost Pack? The free shifter pack?" Sariah's voice broke on a whisper. "It's real?"

Tears glistened in her eyes, which were huge and round, shining in the dim moonlight. Rhys looked down at her, and I could see the exact moment he caved.

"Yeah." He reached over to ruffle her hair, a gesture of sweet familiarity. "It's real, Sah. You want to go there? Meet other shifters?"

She nodded quickly, her eyes lighting up.

"You think the others would come too?" Noah asked.

"I... I think so. They'll want to stick together."

"We need to check everyone for trackers first. Shit, we need to do that now." West's brows drew together.

Sariah looked at him quizzically. "Trackers?"

"Implants under the skin that send a signal back to Strand."

She shook her head. "You can check if you want, but I don't think they put trackers in any of us." Her voice softened almost to a whisper. "Most of the shifters at that facility didn't live long enough to make it worth it."

My thoughts turned to Julie, and I swallowed down a wave of nausea, my heart squeezing with grief. Whatever Strand had been testing at that facility, it hadn't been working.

Pain flashed across Rhys's face as he watched his sister. Then he forced a small smile and put a hand on her shoulder. "Come on, Sah. Let's go tell them about the Lost Pack."

The two of them walked toward the gathered wolves, who lifted their heads as they approached. I hoped the Salt Lake pack would agree to come—leaving them behind would be like leaving them to die. Not that our plan was a guarantee of security, but at least there was safety in numbers. And I'd known my mates long enough to have seen how good they were at surviving against the odds.

West cocked his head to listen to his earpiece before walking a short distance away, staring out at the horizon as he waited for Carl.

Noah and Jackson both turned to me, letting out twin exhales.

"You did it, Scrubs." Noah used his knuckle to raise my chin slightly, his gray-blue eyes shining. "You called your wolf when you needed her. And you let her fight. You're half the reason we made it out of there alive."

I didn't believe that for one minute, but my wolf practically purred at the compliment. There was still a divide between us, a gap that existed between her and me, but there were more and more places where we overlapped. Someday, maybe, we would truly become one.

"Complete and total fuckin' badass." The brown-haired shifter tugged me into his arms, using the pad of his thumb to swipe away a smear of blood from my cheek. But in true Jackson fashion, instead of looking horrified at my grisly state, he looked impressed.

I reached up to grab his forearm, keeping him connected to me for a second longer. I wanted nothing more than to lock myself in a room with my mates for a week, to remind myself why we were doing all of this—of the love and goodness in this world that was worth fighting for.

A low whistle sounded, and I glanced over to see West lift an arm in greeting. Carl and Molly walked out of the darkness toward us, hand in hand.

Jackson made a sound that was almost a growl, eyeballing Carl as they approached. Then he pulled off his bulletproof tactical vest and yanked his shirt over his head, tossing it to me.

I plucked it out of the air gratefully before slipping it on. It barely covered everything, but it was better than nothing. Feeling suddenly self-conscious, I ran the back of my hand over my face, though I knew it was a pretty useless attempt. And Molly, at least, had already seen me covered in blood.

Noah shifted back to wolf form, and the three of us walked forward. When we were halfway to them, Molly broke away from Carl to meet me. She pulled me into a tight hug, ignoring my bloody face and oversized t-shirt.

"God, that was terrifying to hear from the outside. I'm sure it was awful to actually live it." She pulled back. "Are you all right?"

I nodded on autopilot. "Did you guys see any other Strand hunters show up? What's going on at the complex?"

"No more of them. No cops yet either." Carl huffed a breath. "Believe it or not, from topside, it's hard to tell anything really happened. And I know how much shit I sent you down there with. With that amount of explosives, the inside should be pretty well wrecked."

"Thank you." I spoke fervently, even knowing the words would never be enough. "For everything. Thank you both."

A lopsided smile tugged at Carl's mouth. "You know, I didn't just do this because I owe you—even though I do pay all my debts. What Strand's doing isn't right. I've done a few things in my life I'm not proud of. Every once in a while, I like to do the right thing."

Molly rolled her eyes, but neither one of us pointed out that Carl was a much better man than he gave himself credit for.

A faint noise in the distance made me jump, and my attention was drawn to the dark landscape behind them. Despite his reassurances, I still felt on-edge, anxious to get out of here.

"Rhys said maybe you can find a way to get us out of here? *All* of us?" I gestured behind me to the huddled pack.

For a moment, Carl's gaze stuck on the large, shadowy forms of the wolves, a look of awe and disbelief passing over his face. Then he shook his head, bringing his focus back to me.

"Yeah, I do. But I'll warn you, you're probably not gonna like it."

CHAPTER TWENTY-SIX

"This. *This* is why wolves don't road trip."

West's low voice sounded loud as it bounced off the metal walls of the large semi-truck.

I let out a noise that was half chuckle, half groan. "Yup."

Carl hadn't been lying. None of us had liked his solution. But we also hadn't been able to come up with a better way to transport almost thirty shifters several hundred miles.

He and Molly had led us back to where he'd parked the van in a nearly-empty gas station parking lot, and they'd handed off our few belongings. When he'd jerked his chin toward the large semi nearly hidden from view in an ancillary parking lot, my jaw had almost dropped. But the back was spacious enough to accommodate us all, and he'd swapped out the plates for new ones that would run clean. As long as we didn't get pulled over, we should be pretty untraceable.

It was the best option we'd had, though to be honest, I still hated it.

The air outside was cool, but inside the back of the truck, it felt stuffy and warm. For the recently freed shifters, it probably felt horrifyingly like the place they'd just escaped. Sariah had convinced most of them to shift back to human form so we'd all fit easier. A few had refused, but most had surrendered to her gentle prodding.

The dynamic between the Salt Lake shifters was strange. They were a pack, but also... not. I couldn't identify an alpha, and although they seemed to function as a tight-knit group, they each existed in a sort of bubble, separate from the others.

It made sense, I supposed. They'd been forced together by circumstance, but almost nothing about their situation had been natural. I hoped, once we reached the wide open space where the Lost Pack had gone and they were able to run free, things might change for them. So far, I hadn't had a conversation that lasted longer than a few words with any of the rescued shifters. They were all still too shell-shocked for that.

Rhys had insisted on driving again, and none of his pack mates had argued with him. This truck was a beast. Sariah, Jackson, and Noah had hopped into the front with him, but I'd offered to ride in the back with West. I needed to talk to him, and I wasn't sure when we'd have the chance to be alone again.

Or *somewhat* alone, anyway.

I kind of wished a bunch of strangers weren't sitting around us for this conversation—but then again, it was pretty self-involved of me to imagine that anything I said would be more meaningful or important to them than their own private pain.

In the darkness, I couldn't see West, but I could feel him next to me. A few centimeters separated our arms from touching, and I wondered if that space was deliberate.

Gathering my courage, I cleared my throat. "Um, West?"

"Yeah, Scrubs?"

His use of the nickname the guys had adopted for me warmed my chest, and I forged ahead. "Jackson told me... about what happened to you in San Diego. About the forced mate bond."

There was a pause. "Oh."

"He didn't tell me everything!" I added hastily. "No details. Just that it happened."

"Right."

Even without touching him, I could tell his muscles had just bunched up with tension. I knew he didn't want to talk about it, but I had to get this out.

"West, the thing is—" A lump caught in my throat, and I blew out a slow breath before continuing. "I don't know what Strand did to you. I hope someday you'll trust me enough to tell me, but if you don't or can't, I'll accept that too. But I *need* you in my life. More than I need food or air, it sometimes feels like."

I pulled my twisting fingers apart, sliding one hand along the smooth metal of the truck bed until it brushed against West's. His arm jerked, but he didn't pull away.

"I love you, West. Somewhere in the middle of all this running and hiding and fighting, I fell in love with all four of you. You're my mates, but it's even bigger than that. It's *you*." Tears tracked down my cheeks, but I didn't bother to wipe them away. No one could see them in the darkness anyway. My chest ached as I said the next words, but I somehow kept my voice steady. I needed to make sure he understood. "I love you. And I'll always want more. I want everything. But if that's not what you want, I won't push you. I just need to have you in my life. Even if it's just as—as a friend."

He pulled in a shuddering breath beside me, and I was pretty sure he was crying too. Then his large hand enveloped mine, squeezing tightly.

"I want more too, Scrubs," he murmured, his voice thick. "I want you so much it's all I can think about sometimes. But the mate bond... what Strand did... it fucked me up. I'm so... fucked up." He sighed, turning toward me slightly. "I'll try. I'll keep trying. But I just need time."

My heart cracked open at the pain in his voice, at the doubt that underscored it. His unspoken words lingered between us, and I heard them—felt them—as clearly as if they'd been said aloud.

He might not ever be ready.

"It's okay, West. You have all the time in the world. I'm not going anywhere." I laced my fingers with his as I spoke, tightening my grip on his hand as if to prove my point.

His heavy exhale whispered through the quiet confines of the truck, and when I rested my head on his shoulder, he leaned his head against mine. I let that small contact soothe me, closing my eyes and sinking into it.

I hadn't been lying. I would always want more from him.

The mate bond, and the love I felt for these men, made me crave everything about them.

I wanted his heart. His body. His soul.

But for now, I had a little piece of him back. I had this. And that would have to be enough.

CHAPTER TWENTY-SEVEN

"Are you sure this isn't a huge fucking mistake?" Jackson asked for the third time as we made our way through the pine forest in northern Montana.

"No." Rhys's answering growl was gruff and to the point, but I was pretty sure he spoke for us all.

He'd accurately summed up *my* feelings, anyway.

After driving through the dawn and into the day, we had abandoned the truck by the roadside more than a dozen miles from our final destination. Jackson had eagerly volunteered to "take care of it," but the other three had shut him down quickly, thank goodness. After witnessing the fireball a van was capable of producing, I really didn't want to find out what kind of fireball a massive semi-truck would create.

Most of the Salt Lake pack had shifted back to wolf form as soon as we'd left the cramped confines of the flatbed, and they padded along in a loose cluster around us.

I'd changed into a new set of clothes from one of the bags

Carl and Molly had delivered and used Jackson's old shirt to clean off my face as best I could, but I still felt pretty ragged. It felt like blood had seeped into my pores, and I was desperate for a shower—a craving I tried to curb, reminding myself it might be weeks or months before I had access to those kinds of amenities again.

"Should we not have come?" Sariah cast a scared gaze over the five of us, and Rhys slipped an arm around her shoulders, tugging her toward him.

"Don't worry about it, Sah. It'll all be okay."

I tried not to stare at their interaction, but it was hard not to. I'd seen Rhys's softer side on occasion, but for the most part, I was used to his hard outer shell.

Watching him with Sariah, though—the way he kept an eye on her at all times, the way his voice shifted when he talked to her, the deep register becoming soft and reassuring—made something warm and gooey spread in my chest. He seemed to fill the role of part-brother, part-parent, and judging by the concern in his gaze when he looked at her, he was worried about what all those years held captive by Strand had done to her.

I hadn't known his sister before all this, not like he had. But even I could tell there was something missing, something a little off in her demeanor. As though a part of her hadn't come with us when we'd left the Salt Lake complex. I could only hope that as the reality that she truly was free began to sink in and she got reacquainted with her brother, she'd come out of her shell and find some kind of peace.

Not an easy task. I think we all know that firsthand.

My gaze met West's, and although I could still see a deep sadness in his dark brown eyes, he didn't turn away from me.

Noah took my hand, picking up our flagging pace with a determined stride. "Rhys is right. And if it's not okay, we'll come up with a new plan. We've gotten pretty good at that over the years."

"That's the fucking truth," Jackson agreed with a chuckle. "Hey, remember that time after we first got to Vegas? When West decided the best way for us to make a living was by becoming strippers?"

"It was just a suggestion," West grumbled, his dark skin flushing slightly.

"Uh, sure it was, buddy. You had the playlist and tear-away pants allll ready to go."

I hid my smile behind my hand, sharing a look with Sariah. For a brief moment, I got a glimpse of the girl she might've once been, vivacious and full of life. Then her eyes darkened again, and she dropped her gaze.

"Well, I still maintain we could've made at least as good of money as we did in our other jobs," West insisted.

"Yeah, sure. But we wouldn't have picked up any useful skills." Jackson laughed. "Knowing how to pick locks and hot-wire cars has saved our bacon a bunch of times. How would you have stopped the blond Terminator if all you knew how to do was strip? Give him a lap dance?"

West rolled his eyes, shoving Jackson's shoulder. The brown-haired shifter stumbled sideways a few steps before bouncing back to continue teasing his pack mate.

I lost myself in the comforting sound of their banter and

the steady rhythm of our footsteps as my mind drifted back to Molly and Carl. As concerned as I was about me and my mates, I hoped the two of them would be all right too. I'd hugged the sweet blonde nurse so hard before we left that I'd probably bruised her ribs, and she'd hugged me back just as fiercely.

Somehow, through all of this, she'd become like a sister to me. And despite the differences in our situations, one thing we had in common was that we each knew where our homes were—and it had nothing to do with a physical location.

My gaze drifted over my four mates, my four rescuers.

My home.

No matter what the universe had in store for us, I had to believe that as long as we were together, we stood a chance of overcoming it.

WITH SUCH A LARGE GROUP, many of whom were in shock and slightly malnourished, our progress through the pine forest was slow. At least this time we knew exactly where we were going, thanks to Val's coordinates.

We were about a mile away from our destination when howls in the distance split the quiet air. Our entire party froze in place, cocking our heads to listen. Then, as one, the Salt Lake City pack tipped their heads back and added their voices to the haunting song.

Goose bumps prickled along my skin as the sound permeated my ears, heart, and soul. It was beautiful and sad, hopeful and melancholy. The she-wolf inside me lifted her head at the call.

Then, from the forest ahead of us, four large wolves emerged. The leader shifted in mid-stride, becoming a woman with long auburn hair, hazel eyes, and a wickedly curved scar along the right side of her face.

Val.

Her bearing was confident and strong, her expression severe. But as she neared us, taking in the multitude of wolves around us with a sweep of her gaze, her lips parted in a broad smile.

"Ho-ly fuck." She shook her head with grudging respect, her eyes glinting. "You did it."

"We told you we would." Rhys put his arm around Sariah's shoulders protectively, shooting an almost challenging look at Val.

"That you did, shifter. That you did."

The fierce woman looked almost wistful, as though she was sorry she'd missed out on the fight. I wondered for the first time what might've happened if Nils and his hunters hadn't tracked us to the Lost Pack's previous location and attacked the camp. Rhys had intended to ask Alpha Elijah whether he'd allow members of his pack to help us if they chose, but we'd been forced to run for our lives before he could get an answer.

Would Val have volunteered? Would any of the other Lost Pack wolves have stepped forward?

Val's assessing gaze took in the new shifters with us, noting their dull fur and thin frames. Her face hardened with anger at the pitiful sight as her three shifter guards walked among us, sniffing at the newcomers.

"And I'm guessing these are others from the same complex where you found your sister?"

Rhys nodded.

The auburn-haired woman stepped forward, completely unfazed by her nakedness. Her long hair fell over her shoulders and breasts, and somehow, even without a stitch of clothing or armor on, she looked like a fucking warrior.

She raised her voice, addressing the crowd. "You are all welcome here. The Lost Pack has been, and always will be, a safe haven for escaped shifters. Please, come with me."

With a jerk of her chin, she signaled to her guard. They fanned out around us, two on each side and one bringing up the rear. Val fell into step with us as we resumed walking, turning her head to look from me to my men. Her expression grew grave, and she lowered her voice.

"I'm glad to see you alive. But I have to warn you, not everyone may share that sentiment. Alpha Elijah still blames you for the ambush of our pack. His paranoia kept us prepared for attacks, so our losses weren't as devastating as they could have been. But we did lose several beloved members, and because of the alpha's influence, other pack members may blame you too."

Guilt twisted my stomach. It was hard not to agree with Alpha Elijah's assessment. Our arrival had been the thing that led Strand hunters right to the Lost Pack's doorstep. The fact that we didn't know, that we'd never intended to bring that kind of danger with us, was irrelevant in the end. It didn't change what had happened.

"I don't think he'll deny you entry." Val glanced back over her shoulder, taking in the group behind us. "Especially not with so many in need. But I thought you should know what kind of reception to expect."

"Thanks." West's brows drew together, his face tightening with concern. "We'll talk to him."

"All of us except Rhys," Jackson joked, although I was sure he absolutely meant it. "He already pissed the alpha off bad enough. Maybe he should just keep his mouth shut."

"I have nothing to say to him," Rhys said flatly.

Vivid memories of our first time meeting Alpha Elijah filtered through my mind, and the worry in my gut intensified. Rhys had clashed with the stoic, immovable man almost immediately, and things had only gone downhill from there. He might say he had no words for the alpha, but how long would that last?

"Good." Jackson chuckled. "'Cause the only things I imagine you want to say to him would probably burn all the hair off his ears."

"We'll have to be smart about this," Noah put in. "We need to—"

He broke off as we crested a small rise and finally got a look at what lay beyond. The previous Lost Pack location had been a strange sort of makeshift village built into the forest, with crude structures that only vaguely resembled huts.

But this?

This was something else entirely.

"What...?" I breathed, staring at the large array of buildings before me.

"It's an abandoned military base," Val filled in. "There's no electricity, so most of the facilities don't work, but it's a roof over our heads, at least. And it hides us better from aerial view."

I nodded, my gaze still locked on the base. It looked unnervingly like the kind of compound we'd just rescued Sariah and the other shifters from, and I had to remind myself that there was nothing to fear inside those walls. This wasn't Strand.

We walked the rest of the way in silence, all of us on high alert, bodies tense and ears pricked. Finally, we reached the edge of the compound, following a path between two large gray buildings. Lookouts must've seen us coming, because before we made it more than a few yards, Alpha Elijah appeared, striding quickly toward us.

He took in our whole party with a sweeping gaze before his penetrating stare settled on Noah, Jackson, West, Rhys—and finally, on me. Val stepped forward to speak low in his ear, gesturing to us as she did. The middle-aged man's eyes widened, then narrowed. He swept a hand through his shaggy brown hair, his thick beard quivering as he clenched his teeth.

We all waited in silence. Not even Rhys spoke.

For several long moments, the alpha glowered at us, brows drawn together over his dark blue eyes. I tried to keep my expression neutral, but I could feel the muscles of my legs and shoulders tensing, preparing to run or fight. I wiped my sweaty palms on my pants.

Shit. He's not going to let us stay.

But would he let us leave? Now that we'd seen the Lost Pack's new location, would he risk letting us go? Risk Strand capturing us again and using us to track them down?

Finally, when I thought my heart was going to pound right out of my chest, the alpha blinked. Then he lifted his head, raising his booming voice.

"No shifter who seeks asylum with the Lost Pack will ever be denied. You are all welcome here. Even those of you for whom this is a *second chance*."

His dark tone didn't match his civil words, and instead of saying anything else, he pivoted on his heel and strode away.

Val returned to us, cocking an eyebrow as if to say, *I warned you.*

I let out a shuddering breath, nodding in acknowledgment. At least she *had* warned us, although it was too late to change course now. She gestured us forward, and we continued through the abandoned base, the wolves behind us snuffling and whining nervously as Lost Pack shifters stopped in their tracks to watch us pass by.

I could feel their gazes on us like scorching spotlights, following our slow progression through the camp. Whispers and murmurs buzzed in our wake as the onlookers' expressions morphed from surprise into resentment, anger, and fear.

Noah slipped his hand into mine, lacing our fingers together, and Rhys grabbed my arm protectively. He kept

Sariah close on his other side as Jackson and West crowded behind us, eyeing the Lost Pack shifters warily.

The tension that had been winding through my stomach settled into a hard knot.

We'd promised the Salt Lake City pack they would be safe here. And they would. I had to believe that. But a nagging voice inside me kept asking the same question over and over again.

Had we brought them into an even more dangerous situation than the one they'd been in before?

THANK YOU FOR READING!

I absolutely loved writing this book, and I hope you loved reading it just as much! If you did, please leave a review (even a sentence or two makes a huge difference!).

And don't worry, I won't leave you hanging! Book three, *Wolf Claimed,* is coming soon.

In the meantime, you can dive into my complete reverse harem urban fantasy series, *Magic Awakened*, starting with the free prequel novella, *Kissed by Shadows*.

Join my mailing list at sadiemossauthor.com, and I'll send you your FREE copy of *Kissed by Shadows*!

Made in United States
Cleveland, OH
14 March 2026